"That Is Blasphemy!" Said the Rabbi.

"You are not God. You cannot play like this with creation!"

The rabbi stepped back. His eyes were bright with rage. He lifted his cane and pointed it at Vörös.

For a moment nothing happened. Then the world exploded. The forest tore free of the sky, and the sun skittered away like a top. Kicsi held on tightly to the rock and closed her eyes. A noise filled the world, drowning it in thunder, and went on and on forever. She lived alone in an agony of darkness and sound. She opened her eyes.

Vörös lay on the ground, not moving.

THE RED MAGICIAN

Lisa Goldstein

A TIMESCAPE BOOK
PUBLISHED BY POCKET BOOKS NEW YORK

Another *Original* publication of TIMESCAPE BOOKS

A Timescape Book published by
POCKET BOOKS, a Simon & Schuster division of
GULF & WESTERN CORPORATION
1230 Avenue of the Americas, New York, N.Y. 10020

ISBN: 0-671-41161-6

First Timescape Books printing January, 1982

10 9 8 7 6 5 4 3 2 1

POCKET and colophon are trademarks of Simon & Schuster.

Use of the TIMESCAPE trademark is by exclusive license from Gregory Benford, the trademark owner.

Printed in the U.S.A.

*To my parents, Harry and Miriam,
and to Grace Rose Gabe*

THE RED
MAGICIAN

Chapter

1

In the town where Kicsi grew up there was a rabbi who could work miracles. It was a small town, and borders—Hungarian, Czech, Russian—ebbed and flowed around it like tides. Once, Kicsi remembered, she went too far from home and came to a place where the people spoke a different language. In the distance, on the horizon, stood the mountains, fat and placid as cows.

The rabbi who could work miracles was sitting in the living room talking to her parents as Kicsi came down the stairs early one morning. Outside the sun was rising slowly, its light falling on the trees and fields and the high tops of the brown and gray houses. Everything was silent, expectant, as though the town were spinning itself a tight cocoon of wool, preserving itself intact for future generations. The birds sounded muffled and far away.

"I'm sorry," Imre, Kicsi's father, was saying, "I don't agree with you. I don't see the point. Why should you—" He broke off as Kicsi came into the room. "Good morning, Kicsi," he said.

"Hurry and eat your breakfast," said Sarah, Kicsi's mother. "All the others have eaten and you'll be late for school."

"Let her stay," said the rabbi. "This concerns her too. She will not be going to school."

"Not going—" said Kicsi. "But why? What has happened?"

The rabbi leaned forward onto his walking stick to face her. The tips of his white beard nearly touched his knees. "You see," he said, "I've heard that the Hebrew language is being taught there as if it were Yiddish or—or Magyar. Is this true?"

Bits of Hebrew conversation came to her. My house, your house, our house. Hello, how are you? "Yes, it is," she said. "But we learn other things too. We learn—"

"They speak Hebrew now in Palestine, the immigrants," said Imre. "The school is keeping up with the times."

"Palestine," said the rabbi. "Immigrants." He scowled. Kicsi played nervously with a fold in her dress. "You see," said the rabbi, "Hebrew will be spoken only when the Messiah comes and we return to the Holy Land. That is to say, when God wills it. Until then Hebrew is to be spoken only in prayer.

"You must not send your children to this school, Imre," he went on. "They blaspheme against the Holy Name."

Imre looked at the rabbi. He was obstinate. He had been obstinate even as a young man, when he had overheard his parents making plans for his future. "And Imre," his father had said, "I think Imre will study to be a butcher." The young man had been so horrified at this that he had run away from his village. Twenty years later he had a house and a printing company next door.

"I want to give my children a good Jewish education," he said now. "Where else could I send them?"

"At the school they will learn only lies and half-truths about their traditions," said the rabbi. "You could teach them better yourself, at home. For reading and mathematics and so forth they could go to the public school."

"I don't agree," said Imre. "Kicsi is thirteen, too old to be taught at home. And the rest of my children are older. They will continue to go to the school."

The rabbi looked out the window. The only things that moved outside were shadows and chimney smoke. He raised his heavy eyebrows and turned to Imre. "I'm afraid not," he said. "You see, I will put a curse on the school."

Imre moved awkwardly in his chair. Sarah, watching

him, felt a touch of terror at the rabbi's words. Five years ago Imre had gone to Budapest to have a delicate operation on his spine, and Sarah, fearing that he would die, had asked the rabbi to pray to God to save him. The operation had been successful, but Imre had lost the use of his left arm.

"I am telling you this," the rabbi went on, "because you are one of the most influential people in the town. If you take your children out of the school, the rest of the townspeople will soon do the same."

"I'm not afraid of your curses," Imre said finally. "My children will continue to go to the school."

"You will delay things for a while," said the rabbi. "But the school will die all the same. Soon your children will be the only ones attending."

He grasped his walking stick and stood up. "No need," he said, as Imre stood to walk him to the door. "I hope you'll reconsider. Good day." He opened the door and let himself out.

Kicsi ran to Sarah and held her. "What will happen?" she asked. "Can he kill us? What will he do?"

"Hush," said Sarah, still badly frightened herself. "You shouldn't let the devil hear you say such things or they may come true. Everything will be all right."

Kicsi hugged Sarah tightly. The overstuffed chair smelled of lavender and chamomile.

"Hush," said Sarah again. "Now, go to school."

"Cursed be the school," said the rabbi. "And cursed be those who go there to study, and cursed be those who send their children there to study. Forty demons will dwell with them for forty days and nights, and their life will be filled with torment. And cursed be those who talk to them, and those who call on them, and those who sit at their table. Twenty demons will dwell with them for twenty days and nights, and they will have no peace.

"And thrice cursed be those who teach at the school, for they have blasphemed. From them the Holy Name has turned His face, and they are damned eternally."

The rabbi paused. He remembered vividly the time Sarah had come to see him, her look of helplessness and the quick grateful smile she had given him when he had promised to pray for her and her husband. He felt no anger against them now. Well, perhaps Imre would change his mind. He sighed and said, "Amen."

A few blocks away, Kicsi was working a different kind of magic. While walking home from school she had seen a nun, and she knew that if she made a wish and held the top button of her shoe until she saw a chimney sweep her wish would come true. Her arm hurt from stretching it and her legs were beginning to cramp, but she held on to the button as if it were a life raft. She wiped the hair from her face with her free hand as she looked hopefully up at the street, but she saw only a few students. Sighing, she lowered her head and looked again at her shoe, a hand-me-down from an older sister.

She was not quite sure what she had wished for. She knew it had to do with words—words that conjured up other words within her mind. Siam: silk, spices, tea, houseboats and jungles and sand under moonlight. Arabia: camels, figs, dates, leagues of desert sand, women with their faces hidden by veils of old coins. Paris, New York: fashionable dresses and silk stockings and more automobiles than she had seen in a lifetime.

Beyond the mountains, she knew, were other people, other ways of life. Her father had left his town, had escaped and made a new life; she wanted her turn. In her mind the suitcases were all packed, the good-byes all said. She was ready to leave, ready for whatever fate would send her.

She looked up again. There! It was a chimney sweep, unmistakable, covered with soot. She straightened slowly, stretched her legs, and flexed her fingers. She smiled with triumph.

That Friday at the synagogue Imre met a stranger. In a town where everyone knew everyone else the stranger stood out. He was tall, with bright red hair and beard, and his clothes—Imre did not recognize the fashion, but they were clearly not from Eastern Europe. Imre noticed the man during the services and planned to talk to him later and make him feel welcome, after he had talked for a while with the other men in the village as he had done every week for most of his life. But after the services the other men backed away when he approached them, smiling and nodding and making excuses about an early dinner. Word of the curse had spread. The school was half empty, and the parents of the children who remained were nervous and ready to change sides.

Finally only Imre and the stranger were left, standing in the shadows of the synagogue. The lamplighter made his slow way down the street, casting light against darkness.

"Sholom aleichem," said Imre. "Where are you from?"

"Aleichem sholom," said the stranger. "Lately? Lately I'm from Czechoslovakia." Imre couldn't place his accent. It wasn't Czech or Slovak.

"Ah," said Imre. "Czechoslovakia. When this town was part of Czechoslovakia, those were better times. The freedom—"

"You wouldn't recognize Czechoslovakia now," said the stranger. "The freedom is gone now—the Germans have seen to that."

"The Germans," said Imre. "The Hungarian government signed a treaty with the Germans, only last year. But so far they have not acted against us." He shrugged with his right arm, his left arm a dead weight against his side. "We are such a small village, after all, and so far from things . . ."

A look, almost of pain, crossed the stranger's face, but he said nothing. Sudden alarm took Imre. "Do you think— Are we in danger?" he asked.

"I think—perhaps you are," the stranger said softly. "But perhaps not for a while. Still, if you have relatives in America"—he glanced at Imre, and Imre found himself wondering how the stranger had known about his family —"you should make plans to leave this place."

"To—to leave?" Imre said. "To leave my village?"

"If you can," said the stranger. "But come, my friend, let's talk of more cheerful subjects."

"So," said Imre, saying the first thing that came into his mind, "are you planning to stay here awhile?"

"No," said the stranger. "Only for a few days."

"Do you have a place to stay?"

"No."

"Then I insist you stay with us," said Imre. "Though I should warn you—we've had a disagreement with the rabbi. And the townspeople, for the most part, have sided with him."

"Your rabbi," the stranger said. "They say he's a great scholar, or so I've heard."

13

"He was at one time," Imre said. "And perhaps he still is. Though I find myself disagreeing with him more and more."

"Well, then," said the stranger. "I would like to stay with you very much. What the rabbi thinks of you is not my concern."

"Good, very good," said Imre. "What is your name?"

"By my friends I am called Vörös," said the stranger. *Vörös* means red or redhead in Hungarian.

"Very good. Let's go home."

So, Imre thought, glancing at the tall man beside him as they set off through the evening streets, you don't want me to know your name or your business. Very well. You didn't want to know my business with the rabbi and the people of the village. You could be a political prisoner, escaped from those dogs in Germany, or you could be running guns to Palestine. Perhaps, perhaps. You could—who knows?—steal my silverware or one of my daughters, or murder me in my sleep. But I think not. I think you are an honest man, Vörös, and I think your business is your own.

The shadows were lengthening and the streets almost deserted as Imre and Vörös came home. *"Gut Shabbos,* Sarah," said Imre. "I have brought a guest. This is Vörös."

"Come in, come in, Vörös," said Sarah. "Girls, one of you run and get another plate for our guest. We have company!"

Kicsi turned and saw the stranger in the doorway. Light from the house fell upon him, turning his beard and hair golden. He looked at her, and she thought that he could not be much older than Magda, the oldest sister. His skin was pale and his eyes in the light were very blue.

At dinner the girls made much of the stranger, laughing and softly teasing him about his hair. Their brother Tibor sat near Imre and watched Vörös quietly. "Where are you from?" asked Magda.

Vörös repeated his words to Imre. "Lately? Lately from Czechoslovakia."

"No," said Kicsi. "Where were you before that?"

Imre shot her a warning glance, but she ignored it and looked instead directly at Vörös.

"All over," Vörös answered, smiling. "Europe, America, Asia . . ."

"Asia!" said Kicsi, breathing the word, savoring it.

"He means Palestine," said Ilona scornfully. "No one goes any farther than that."

"No," said Vörös. "I've been to Palestine, certainly, but I've been farther. Shanghai."

Shanghai. It was another word for Kicsi to store away and save, to bring out later and examine. This, then, was the way her wish would be answered. "Where else?" she said. "What was it like? Did you see statues and ruins and bazaars? Did you go to the Great Wall of China? To the Himalayas?"

Vörös laughed. "Yes, yes, all of that and more," he said.

"What did—" She stopped, noticing for the first time the thin scar that ran from his hairline, cutting across one eyebrow and disappearing into his beard. "Where did you get that scar?"

"Kicsi!" said Imre.

"It's all right," said Vörös. "I don't mind. It was during the last war. We were attacked by looters."

"The war?" said Kicsi suspiciously. "You're not old enough."

"Now that is really enough, do you hear me!" said Imre. "Excuse my daughter, please. She sometimes gets carried away."

"Oh, she doesn't bother me," said Vörös. "I'd be happy to answer her questions." Then, seeing Imre's expression: "Some other time, perhaps."

The next day Kicsi found Vörös seated at a table, looking through the books in the library. "Tell me a story," she said.

Vörös put down the book he was holding. His hands, Kicsi noticed, were pale and slender, and covered with fine golden hair. "What kind of story?" he asked.

"Anything," said Kicsi fiercely.

"Let me see," said Vörös. Kicsi watched him carefully, studying his smooth young face, his clear wide eyes, his short curly beard. "All right. When I was in America I worked for a while for a magician."

"Really?"

"Yes, a real magician. He looked like a cat—like an old cat that's been left out in the rain too long, sort of seedy and mangy—but you knew that he'd always find enough to eat, and somehow, no matter where we were, he'd always manage to keep himself spotlessly clean. He had long sleek black hair, and an elaborately curled black mustache, but under the mustache all his teeth were rotten. We'd travel around from town to town, putting on shows, and once a year we'd return to New York.

"He loved New York. I don't know why. New York is dirty and noisy and crowded, and likely to get worse. But he seemed very much at home there, and he'd always tell me, after a particularly good night, that when he'd had enough of touring he'd settle down in New York and never go back on stage again.

"Well, one night in New York we'd done fairly well. He'd taught me a few tricks with coins and flowers and cards—"

"Can you still do them?" said Kicsi.

"Surely. You never forget. I'll show you a few, after the Shabbos. Anyway, toward the end of the show we did a vanishing act. What usually happened was, I'd build a box around the magician, made of thick boards, and when I opened the box he would be gone. Then I'd close up the box, open it again, and—lo and behold—there he'd be again. But this particular night, when I opened the box again, he was still missing. I was panicked. The audience got restless, and then furious. Then they began to throw things. I hurried off the stage. But as I left, I swore I saw a sleek black cat walking out the stage door."

Kicsi thought awhile. "That's not a true story," she said finally.

"Well, you know how stories are. Parts of them are true and parts are made up. And anyway, you didn't ask me for a true story."

"Kicsi!" someone called.

"That's Magda," said Kicsi. "I'd better go."

"Come back any time," said Vörös. "We'll talk some more."

"I will," said Kicsi.

The next day Kicsi waited impatiently for school to end. The few students that remained fidgeted restlessly, certain the curse was coming home to rest on their shoulders. They were afraid to stay in school and afraid to disobey their parents by leaving. The teachers could do nothing with them. Kicsi, unnoticed, sat in a corner and daydreamed of Vörös.

She ran home after school, stopping for no one. He wasn't there. All afternoon she waited, wandering through the old, vast house until at last she heard his footsteps at the door. She ran to the living room.

"Vörös!" she said. "Tell me a story."

"Give me a minute, please," said Vörös. He sighed and sat in one of the chairs, stretching his long legs in front of him. "I have a better idea. Why don't you tell me a story?"

"Me?" said Kicsi. "About what? I haven't been anywhere."

"Oh, about anything," Vörös said. "Why do they call you Kicsi, for example?"

"Oh, that," Kicsi said. "That's not important. They've called me the Little One since I was born. Because I'm the youngest. My real name is—"

"No," said Vörös. "If you tell me your real name I shall have to tell you mine. Tell me something else. What did you do in school today?"

"Well," said Kicsi. She thought awhile. "The school is under a curse."

"A curse?" said Vörös.

"Yes. Because they teach Hebrew, and the rabbi says no one can speak Hebrew until the Messiah comes. So he cursed it."

"Really? Can he do that?"

"I suppose he can," said Kicsi. It no longer seemed as important. "A lot of people think he can, anyway. There's almost no one left in the school.

"Wait a minute," said Kicsi suddenly. "Do you think he's wrong? Maybe the Messiah's come and no one has noticed yet. Do you think so? You've been to Palestine— maybe you've seen him there and didn't know it."

Vörös laughed. "No, I don't think so," he said. "When the Messiah comes, everything will be different. Elijah the Prophet will walk into Jerusalem and the Messiah, the son of David, will follow him. Then the air will be like myrrh and cinnamon, and the rivers will run with honey. The Temple will stand where it stood of old, built of gold and cedar wood and ivory. All promises will be fulfilled and all questions answered. We will come from the four corners of the earth, and the graves will give up their dead, and we will meet in the Promised Land and rejoice." He sounded wistful, as though recalling a dream. "Didn't the rabbi tell you that?"

"No," said Kicsi. "He just tells us what we can't do."

"Oh, now," said Vörös. "He can't be that bad."

"You don't know him," said Kicsi. It was strange to think that she had stood in almost the same place a few days ago and the rabbi had leaned on his walking stick to talk to her. "I don't like him at all."

A crystal candlestick holder fell off the mantel onto the wooden floor and broke into a thousand pieces. Vörös half-stood, then sat back in his chair.

"Kicsi!" Sarah shouted from the kitchen. Kicsi heard hurrying footsteps and then Sarah came into the room. "What did you do?"

"I—it just fell. I didn't do it. I didn't do anything."

"That's right," said Vörös. "It just fell to the floor."

Sarah saw Vörös for the first time. "Didn't your father say you weren't to talk to him?" she said to her daughter. "Now go. Get the broom and clean up this mess, and then come help me in the kitchen. And I don't want to catch you talking to Vörös again. Do you hear me?"

"But—"

"No buts. Do as I say." Sarah left the room.

Slow tears formed in Kicsi's eyes. She went to get the broom and began to sweep, slowly, methodically. The pieces of crystal blurred and ran together, sparkling. Suddenly she turned to Vörös, leaning forward on the broom.

"When are you leaving?" she asked.

"In—" He cleared his throat. "In a few days."

"Take me with you."

"What? I can't. Why?"

"I want to leave home. I'm almost an adult, you know. They treat me like a child because I'm the youngest. They don't know. I want to see faraway places, I want to do things—I want to be like you."

"Faraway places? What do you know of faraway places?" Vörös moved forward in his chair. "All too soon you will leave this place, your village. You will go through pain and fire and hunger, and I cannot say what the end will be. It may be that you will finally come to Palestine, or to America. And there you will tell your children stories of your childhood, and they will think this town as exotic, as far away, as Shanghai. And all too soon they will want to leave you for faraway places. Things happen, you know. You cannot rush them."

She looked at him in amazement. America! What did he mean? "I don't understand," she said.

Magda came into the room, turned slowly in a circle to look at both of them, and ended by looking at the broken glass. "Mother's very upset about something," she said. "She said you're to clean that up and then go help her. I'm supposed to make sure that you do it. What did you do, knock it over?"

Kicsi said nothing. She resumed sweeping, quietly. After a while Vörös cleared his throat, interrupting the rustling of the broom and the clinking of glass. He stood, walked to the door, and let himself out into the cool evening. Kicsi never looked around.

She didn't see him for nearly a week. She suspected some conspiracy between Vörös and Sarah, designed to keep them apart for the time he was staying. The next Friday at dinner time, however, he came in with Imre. She was helping to set the table. As she saw him, her heart leapt like a salmon from a stream.

"I'm leaving after Shabbos," he told the family, not looking at her. "I came for one final delightful meal."

"Where are you going?" asked Sarah. Kicsi, setting down a wine cup, pretended not to listen to his answer.

"To England, I think," he said. "And then to America."

"We have cousins in America," said Tibor. "In New York. Will you be seeing them?"

"Silly!" said Magda, laughing. "America's a big place. Not like here."

"I *know* that," said Tibor, furious. "I could give him the address—"

The telephone rang. It was the private line, recently installed, that ran from the house to the printing plant next door. Imre looked at his wife.

The phone rang again. One was not allowed to use the telephone on the Shabbos, the day of rest, since the rabbis had ruled that using electricity constituted lighting a fire, which was considered work and so prohibited. But any rule could be sacrificed in an emergency.

"Who can be at the plant at this hour?" asked Imre. "Everyone should have gone home hours ago."

19

The phone rang again. "Perhaps you'd better answer it," said Sarah. "Someone may have gotten locked inside."

Imre went to the phone. "Hello?"

"Hello?" There was an unmistakable sound of relief in the voice at the other end of the phone. "Hello. This is Arpad."

"Arpad?" said Imre. Arpad was an employee at the printing plant, stolid and unimaginative and not very bright. His face was marked with smallpox scars. "What are you doing there?"

"I—I followed a light," said Arpad.

"A light?" said Imre.

"Yes, sir. When we were closing. I was about to leave, as all the lights had been turned off, when I saw this light, sir, and I thought that maybe one of them had been missed. So I went to look, and—and it moved. And I followed it, and it kept moving from room to room, past the presses, and into the offices, and then back to the presses —a sort of thin yellow light, sir. And then finally it went out, and I found the door, and then, well, I was locked in."

"A light?" Imre said again. "I don't understand. Was it someone holding a torch? Do you think he's still there?"

"Oh, no, sir," said Arpad. "It wasn't anyone holding a torch. I would have seen that. It was just a light." He paused. "I'd rather talk about this outside, sir. You see, it's fairly dark in here. I can't seem to get the lights back on, somehow."

"Very well," said Imre. "I'll be coming through the entrance connected to the house. Just wait there."

"Thank you, sir."

Just outside the dining room was a door that led to the plant. "Get me my keys, one of you," said Imre, putting down the phone. "I think I left them upstairs." Ilona ran to the stairs.

"Sarah, tell him I'll have to wait until I get the keys—"

A slow rumbling started. They heard it in two places— over the telephone and from the plant next door.

Magda cried out. Sarah said, "What's that?"

"The fool," said Imre. "He's somehow started the presses."

The sound became a muted roar. Occasionally the clanking rhythm of an individual press could be heard before it faded back into the general noise.

20

"Let me out!" said Arpad. "Please. Help. Let me out!"

Sarah picked up the telephone. "Imre will get you out as soon as he gets the keys," she said. "How did you manage to start the presses?"

"I didn't start them," said Arpad. "They're just going by themselves. I had nothing to do with it."

"God help us," said Sarah. "It's the curse. The rabbi's curse." She sat down, the phone still in her hand, and looked blankly at the connecting door.

Ilona returned with the keys. "Here they are," she said, panting.

Imre fitted the key to the lock. The door began to shake. With his paralyzed left arm he could not hold the door steady.

"The light!" said Arpad. "The light is coming back!"

The door began to swing back and forth, although Imre had not turned the key in the lock. The Shabbos candles flickered. A glass of wine overturned, the stain spreading slowly through the white linen like a fist unclenching.

"Help!" said Arpad. Everyone in the room could hear his thin voice through the telephone. "Help! He's strangling me! I'm being strangled!"

The dinner table began to tremble. Silverware and china rattled like chattering teeth. The candles went out.

"In Heaven's name!" said Vörös. "What does he think he's doing?"

The door closed. Imre fumbled with the lock.

"Please! Somebody! I'm being strangled!"

Vörös ran to the door, pushing Imre out of the way. As the door tore itself loose from the frame once more, Vörös pushed at it with his shoulder. The door flung open. The presses became louder.

Vörös said one word into the din. The word sounded like breath, like wind, like the sea speaking to sand. The presses stopped.

Arpad came to the door. He looked at the family, gathered around him like the crowd that gathers around a man feared dead, and fainted. Imre and Vörös together dragged him to the table.

Imre unbuttoned Arpad's shirt and peeled back the collar. He sucked in his breath in dismay. Standing out against the pale skin were deep red marks, marks like fingers.

"Somebody! Somebody get a doctor," said Imre. "Sarah,

wet a napkin and bring it to me. Stand back, all of you—
he's fainted. You can look at his neck another time. Get
back!"

Kicsi looked, horrified, at the red marks. Slowly she
moved back with everyone else, as Sarah applied the wet
napkin, as Arpad opened his eyes. She looked around for
Vörös. She wanted to ask him if the word he had spoken
was the holy and unutterable Name of God. But Vörös had
gone.

Chapter

2

Kicsi and her best friend, Erzsébet, sat in the attic. Several months had passed since Vörös had left, and summer had come and gone. Dust motes flowed like molten gold through a hole in the roof—a hole that no one had known was there and on which Kicsi and Erzsébet were speculating endlessly.

It was midafternoon. In the huge old house that contained her mother and father, three other children, a visiting cousin from Budapest, and friends and workers from the press who were always stopping by, Kicsi thought she had about an hour before anyone would think of looking for her in the attic. She sat against the wall looking at the old furniture, trunks of clothes and photographs, mirrors gone blind from the dust. Erzsébet stood up and looked through the hole to the street below.

"Maybe this is how Vörös left," Erzsébet said. "Through the roof."

"Don't be silly," said Kicsi. "We were all on the first floor. He would have left a hole in every ceiling he passed through."

"Oh," said Erzsébet dully. The hot sun was making her sleepy.

"And besides," Kicsi said, "someone would have heard him."

"Oh," said Erzsébet. She turned and sat down next to Kicsi. "There sure are a lot of people down on the street."

"There are? Who?"

"Visitors for the rabbi's daughter's wedding, mostly. They're all looking at your house."

Kicsi scowled.

"Well," said Erzsébet, pushing up her glasses, "they want to see the house where the magician stayed, where he fought with the rabbi and won."

"I wish they'd go away," Kicsi said.

"I wish he'd never come," said Erzsébet.

Kicsi looked at her sharply.

"Well," said Erzsébet, "I wish he'd never taken the curse off the school. I hated going back. I hate Hebrew. I wonder if anyone really speaks it or if they're all just pretending."

"I'll bet it was a tree," said Kicsi.

"The hole?"

"Sure. A tree must've fallen on the roof."

"Where's the tree now?"

"Oh," said Kicsi. "I don't know."

"No, it couldn't have been. Say—" Erzsébet broke off as another thought occurred to her. "Do you suppose the *rabbi* made the hole in the roof?"

"The rabbi? As part of the curse, you mean?"

"Sure. The rabbi, or one—you know—one of the demons." She lowered her voice.

"I think you're right. The rabbi's curse. I wonder why no one noticed the hole before. I'm going to have to tell my father about it before the rains start."

"What was it like?" Erzsébet said suddenly.

"What?"

"You know—being under a curse. Were you frightened?"

"No, not really."

"Did you see any demons?"

"No, not at all. The only thing that happened was when the printing presses started. Oh, and a candlestick holder broke once."

"And the hole in the roof."

"And the hole in the roof."

"And that's all? No noises, no strange voices?"

"No." Kicsi was openly scornful now. "Why did you think there would be?"

"Well, my brother, he said—we have an uncle staying with us for the wedding, and my brother told him—well —that there were sparks when Vörös cast out the demon. Blue sparks, and red, and golden. And that the demon let out a shriek—you could hear it as far away as the forest —and flew up the chimney. And that Vörös spun around three times and flew away, over toward Palestine."

Kicsi laughed. "No, it didn't happen like that."

Erzsébet began to laugh with her. "Wait, you haven't heard the funniest part yet. The funniest part was that he said—my brother said—that he knows what he's talking about, because his sister's best friend lives in the house where Vörös stayed."

They both laughed, Erzsébet louder than Kicsi. Erzsébet looked up at the roof. The light coming through the hole had almost disappeared.

"Oh, Kicsi, I'd better go. I'm going to be late for dinner." They stood up and brushed the dust off their clothes. Kicsi lifted the trapdoor, and first she, then Erzsébet, climbed down the ladder.

Kicsi was almost glad to see Erzsébet go. She could not bear to talk of Vörös yet. For her the most important thing that had happened was that he had gone and might not be coming back. The rabbi had abandoned his feud with the school, and the friends of the family were coming back, sheepishly, to renew old ties, but Kicsi cared little for that. She felt that her heart had gone out of her, that never again would she feel so wholly and completely alive. She was thirteen years old.

They passed the library, and Kicsi remembered how Vörös had once sat there and promised to show her card tricks. Her cousin and Imre were talking behind the closed door. The cousin had come to the village for the wedding of the rabbi's daughter and was staying in the room Vörös had once used. He had been the rabbi's student before he and his family had moved to Budapest. Kicsi hated him thoroughly for daring to take Vörös's place and at the same time knew that he had done nothing to deserve her hatred.

"Wait," Kicsi said.

"Wait for what?" said Erzsébet.

"I thought I heard them say my name. Wait just a minute."

"Oh, Kicsi, I really have to go home now."

"All right, go. I have to hear what they're saying."

"Good-bye, Kicsi," said Erzsébet.

"Good-bye," Kicsi said absently.

"The rabbi certainly knows how to stir up this old sleepy town," the cousin was saying. "I've never seen so many people here at one time."

"We have people here from as far away as Russia," said Imre. "The rabbi's a very famous man. Though we've had our differences in the past—"

"He's a strange man," the cousin said. "I remember when I was studying with him. One of the students disagreed with him on some point of Talmudic law—I can't even remember what it was now—and the rabbi threw him out of the classroom. Just like that. And he never let him back, either."

"He likes to think he is responsible for everyone in the village—for what they think and how they speak and what they do," Imre said. "The village is terribly isolated. Old László wanted to start a newspaper once and asked me if I'd print it, but the rabbi was against it and László gave up the idea."

"Then how do you get news here?" said the cousin.

"Well, the radio. On good days, when the signal makes it over the hills. The rabbi really doesn't allow anything else. He's had too much power, with no one to challenge him, for too long."

"Isn't that what your guest tried to do—to challenge him? I wonder how many people are coming to the wedding just because they heard that story."

The cousin had wanted to hear the tale of the rabbi and Vörös ever since he had come to town, but Imre had forbidden everyone to talk about it. Because the cousin was staying with Kicsi's family he had been asked many times by those in the village for his opinion of the two magicians and had had to pretend to knowledge with quiet nods and winks and a general air that he would tell more if he could.

"My own daughters will be marrying soon," said Imre, changing the subject.

The cousin sighed. "How will you ever find husbands for all three of them?"

"I don't think that will be much of a problem," said Imre. "Magda already has a suitor—a very respectable young man—and as for the rest of them, well, I suppose I can arrange something when the time comes."

Kicsi felt her heart pounding. I don't want to be arranged for! she thought wildly. Will Vörös never come and take me away?

"It'll be hard arranging for a husband for Kicsi," said the cousin, as though the force of her thoughts had driven them through the thick wooden door. "She seems to hate everything and everyone."

"Kicsi?" said Imre. "Why do you say that?"

"She certainly has something on her mind," said the cousin. "I can't even get her to say hello to me."

"You have to treat her very carefully," said Imre. "This is a difficult time for her now." He paused. "You were talking before about the strange traveler who stayed with us for a time."

"Yes," said the cousin. Kicsi could almost hear him move forward in his chair, so eager did he sound to hear the story. She moved closer to the door.

"I think Kicsi fell in love with him," said Imre. "She's always had that love of distant places, exotic people. I think she expects him back, and she will be very disappointed. The man has gone away for good."

"But was he a real magician?" said the cousin.

"No, I don't think so," said Imre. "Just a man who had traveled widely. Please don't mention this to Kicsi. In time, I hope she'll get over it."

Kicsi was furious. How dare he tell that unfeeling oaf of a cousin that Vörös was not a magician? And that he would not be coming back?

She ran to the room she shared with Ilona, the next oldest sister. The big gray cat had gotten on the bed again, and she dropped him to the floor without noticing where he landed. Slowly she reached her hand into her pocket, feeling like her oldest sister furtively taking out a pack of cigarettes when she thought that no one was looking. She took out a pack of cards. Her father printed them, and she had taken a set without asking (though he would have given them to her if she had asked) the last time she was in the plant.

She shuffled through the cards, wondering how one did card tricks. Pick a card. Now I will tell you the card you picked. Did Vörös read minds? Did he know she was waiting here for him? She felt lost, cold and alone in the big stone house. Surrounded by her family, she felt separated from everyone. How much longer could she go on like this, listening at doorways, slinking through the old drafty house, turning into a ghost, into wind?

She fingered through the cards without seeing them. Kings, queens, diamonds, hearts fell to the floor to land beside the cat. When would he return to her?

That night she had a dream. There were groups of people, caravans, coming over the distant hills to the wedding. There was a man among them, a tall man with hair the color of a wheat field. She knew that he had been badly hurt once in a soccer game and had had three teeth knocked out. A long scar ran across his upper lip, and to hide it (for he was very vain) he had grown a mustache of the same wheat color as his hair. He had worn the mustache for years. Now they had promoted him, and they had told him that he must shave it off. He had not wanted to, but he had done it, because he had always done as he was told. The scar, he was surprised to see, had faded over the years to a thin, barely noticeable line. He fingered his bare upper lip as he walked along the roads, proud and happy to be a part of a great and worthwhile plan. He was coming over the distant hills, coming with an army at his back, coming not for the wedding, but to destroy—to destroy—

Kicsi woke up suddenly. The sheets were drenched in sweat. She moved cautiously, glancing at her sister in the next bed, an indefinite shape in the moonlight. Good, Kicsi thought. She hadn't screamed in her sleep. She twisted in the bed, trying to get comfortable, trying to remember the shape of the dream. The man had smiled and his mouth had been black, toothless. Is he coming to destroy us? she wondered. Not all people from distant places mean us well, she thought, and turned over a final time and went to sleep.

She did not remember the dream in the morning, but something—a sense of restlessness, of people moving across

the borders—stayed with her through the day. She avoided
Erzsébet after school and walked along the gravel-paved
streets of the town, winding through a maze that seemed
to be drawing her deeper and deeper, in toward its heart.
She passed the synagogue, passed Erzsébet's house, where
her father the doctor practiced, passed the graveyard, and
came to the outskirts of the town, where the old forest
stood. She had been warned about the forest with tales of
ghosts and demons, but she stayed awhile and watched the
green and orange leaves shifting in the sunlight and listened
to the tall trees rustling in the wind, endlessly passing along
the old secrets. Then she retraced her steps and came at
last to the rabbi's house.

It was the day before the wedding. People came and
went, getting ready for the feast to be held there the next
day. She was not the only one to be drawn to the rabbi's
house out of curiosity; a small crowd stood to one side of
the house. The day was growing colder. Clouds moved
quickly across the sky like cards in some trick of sleight
of hand. Mother will be worrying about me, she thought,
but she could not resist joining the crowd of people.

They were watching a juggler. Kicsi stared at him in
wonder. She thought that she had never seen colors as
bright as those of the balls he tossed in the air: the red
like the core of fire, the blue like the depths of the sea, the
white like stars fused together. They shone like jewels. The
juggler reached into the pack on his back, without losing
the fragile clockwork rhythm of the circling balls, and
pulled out a ball black as midnight, which he tossed into
the air to join the dance of the others. She thought she
could see, tiny but precise as a bead of water on a stem of
grass, small white stars arranged around the face of the
ball. And all the while she was thinking those thoughts,
she wondered why it was that no one had yet recognized
him.

She saw that he stood in shadow, and so his hair was
not as bright a red as she remembered, and that he stood
stooped over, so that he seemed not as tall. She saw that he
had fixed everyone's attention on the quick and cunning
work he did with the balls—now tossing one behind his
back, now sending one under his knee—and so ensured that
no one in the crowd watched his face. And yet she knew.
She felt her blood turn to fire. Vörös had come back.

"He'd taught me a few small tricks with coins and flowers and cards," she heard Vörös say, as though he were standing beside her.

"Can you still do them?"

"Of course. You never forget." Then Vörös said, or she thought he said, "Please don't tell anyone that I am here."

She stood silently, watching the balls blur together and come apart again, watching them disappear in one hand and reappear in the other, watching them move so quickly that they seemed to flow like water, and so slowly that they seemed to hang suspended in air. The shadows lengthened. People came and went, stopping to admire and wonder, occasionally adding coins to a growing pile at Vörös's feet. Finally the juggler caught all the balls one by one as they fell, then held out his hand to show that it was empty. There was some applause, and the people dispersed.

Vörös and Kicsi were left alone. The sun sent out one last ray before it disappeared behind the hills, catching Vörös's hair and turning it to gold. Kicsi stood uncertainly as Vörös picked up the coins and put them in his pack. She had imagined their reunion in many ways, but not in this one. She had seen them run together, holding each other and crying out how glad they were to see the other again. Vörös straightened up finally and looked at her. "Hello," he said shyly, and she realized that she did not know him at all.

"Hello," she said. "Why didn't you want me to tell anyone that you were here?"

Vörös smiled. "I'm not a popular man," he said. "Don't you remember? I would not care to be recognized by your rabbi, and especially not on his very doorstep."

"Where have you been? And why did you disappear so suddenly?" I missed you, Kicsi wanted to say, but something in Vörös's face kept her from saying it.

"I can't tell you," Vörös said. Then, seeing her face, he added, "I'm sorry."

"Is it because I'm too young?" she asked fiercely.

"No," he said. "No, of course not. I can't discuss my business with anyone. And I pray to God you need never learn what I have discovered in the places beyond this town."

"Why?" said Kicsi. The evening shadows drew close

around her. She felt suddenly cold. "Why—what have you discovered?"

"You have entirely too much curiosity for someone your age," Vörös said easily. "Say something to me that isn't a question."

"Where are you staying?" said Kicsi. "Oh—I'm sorry. I mean, you can stay with us if you're not busy elsewhere. Oh, no, you can't either. We have a cousin staying with us. He's come for the wedding." She felt hurt, ignored. She searched for more things to tell him. "Oh, and the rabbi's lifted the curse on the school, I think because of what you did. I think he's afraid of you. Can you tell me how you did that?"

"One minute," said Vörös. "That's two questions you've asked me. I'm staying in the forest."

Kicsi's eyes widened as she looked at the stranger she had thought she knew so well. "The forest? What about the—the animals, the ghosts?"

Vörös laughed. "I'm comfortable there," he said. "I earn a few coins with my juggling, and that brings me my food. Now come. Let us say hello to your father. Do you think he will mind one more for dinner?" He slipped his worn pack—the colors of autumn leaves—over his shoulder.

They set off into the gathering darkness. Stray dogs followed them for a while, barking to one another, but Kicsi and Vörös soon left them behind.

Chapter

3

"Where have you been?" said Sarah. Then, seeing Vörös, she stopped. "Oh. *Sholom aleichem.* I'll set another plate. Magda! Where are the girls?"

"Aleichem sholom," said Vörös. "I hope I'm not disturbing you or your family."

"No, not at all," said Sarah. Her eyes shifted warily from Vörös to Kicsi, as though she suspected him of some diabolical conjuring trick that had substituted this demon in place of her daughter. "Magda, set another place, would you? Vörös has come back."

"Vörös!" Magda said. "Hello."

Vörös nodded to her.

"Vörös!" The cousin came downstairs. His eyes gleamed in the candlelight like newly minted coins. "They've been talking of nothing else here since you've gone. Is it true—did you really—" He paused as they all sat down to dinner. "Tell me—that day you stopped the printing presses. How did you do that? Was it—magic?" His tone was slightly mocking, as if he were reminding everyone that he knew more about the world than they did, as if he were daring Vörös to try to fool him as he had fooled the others.

Kicsi wondered why Imre did not forbid the cousin to

ask those questions. She remembered vividly when Imre had refused to let her talk to Vörös and suspected that the cousin was allowed more freedom only because he was older. Later she realized that Imre had not stopped the conversation because he, too, was curious.

"The presses? I think they stopped by themselves. Didn't they?"

"Where did you go that night?" Tibor asked. "Why didn't you say good-bye to us?"

"I had important business. I'm sorry I couldn't have waited to thank you for your hospitality. And Arpad—is he well?"

"He's fine," said Kicsi. "How did you do that this afternoon?"

"The juggling? It's easy. I'll teach you."

"Juggling!" said Tibor. "I didn't know you could juggle."

Vörös started to say something, but Kicsi continued without hearing him. "No, not the juggling," she said implacably. "You talked to me. In my mind. How did you do that?"

There was silence for a long moment. The cousin, fascinated, had forgotten to eat. Finally Imre said, "Now, Kicsi, our guest is tired. You can talk to him some other time."

"He talked to me," she said. "In my mind." She turned to him. "Are you a magician?" she asked. Her voice was sharp with challenge. She felt betrayed by him. He should have been happier to see her. He should have told her more.

Vörös tasted his soup. He looked up at Kicsi and nodded slightly. "I know a few tricks," he said.

There was a long silence. Finally Imre said, "What's the news from the outside world?"

Vörös looked at him levelly. "Not good, my friend. Can you—Are you prepared to leave this place? There are things moving in the outside world that I do not think your village can stand against."

"To leave?" said Imre. "Leave where? Are you sure?"

"Yes," said Vörös. "I'm sure. I'm sorry."

Imre shook his head. "I don't know," he said. "I've lived in this village for a long time. I would like to talk to the rabbi first."

Vörös nodded gravely. The talk turned to the rabbi, his

33

daughter's wedding, the news from Budapest. After dinner Tibor asked to see Vörös juggle, and Vörös got out his pack.

Kicsi leaned forward to examine the balls. They were the same bright colors as she remembered. "Where did you get these?" she asked.

"Istanbul," said Vörös.

"Oh," said Kicsi. All her hostility melted away like ghosts in the sunlight. "Oh. Istanbul."

Imre looked at Vörös sharply. Vörös's warning had troubled him more than he had shown. Now he felt another worry for his youngest daughter. The old magic had returned.

Vörös hurried through his tricks as if aware of the tension in the room. The family watched him, fascinated. For Kicsi it was as fresh as if she were seeing him juggle for the first time. Even Imre looked interested, and rubbed his useless left arm as though it too would soon move in time to the balls.

"Where are you staying?" Imre asked when he had finished.

"In the forest."

"The forest?" said Imre. "For God's sake, why? I insist—you must be our guest."

"No," said Vörös. "I can't. You already have a guest." He nodded to the cousin. "Thank you. I'll be going now."

"Please," said the cousin. "I'd be quite happy sleeping in the living room."

"No," said Vörös again. "I'm comfortable in the forest. Thank you so much for the meal, and for your kind faces. Good evening." He opened the door and stepped out into the night. One of the dogs melted out of the darkness and followed at his heels. Imre tried to contain his feeling of relief.

The next day, after she had come home from school, Kicsi saw Ilona's dress laid out on her bed. "Mother says you're to wear that to the wedding," said Ilona when she returned from her bath. She started to dress.

"I hate it," said Kicsi. "You're too fat. All your dresses are too loose on me."

"I am not too fat," said Ilona, standing by the mirror and breathing out.

"Why don't I ever get my own dresses?" said Kicsi, but it

was an old complaint, and the family had learned to ignore it years ago as they had learned to ignore the background noise of the printing presses. She walked out the door toward the bathroom, trailing the dress behind her.

Later, washed and dressed, Kicsi sat on the bed and arranged and rearranged the cards. She felt uncomfortable in the new dress. The wedding would not start until evening. It was hoped that if the wedding were held under the night sky the children of the bride and groom would be as numerous as the stars in the heavens. Ilona came in the room as Kicsi was staring at the back of a card, willing it to reveal itself to her. Kicsi grabbed for the cards, but it was too late—Ilona had seen them already.

"Whatever are those?" Ilona said.

"Here," Kicsi said, holding the deck out to her clumsily. "Pick a card. Please."

"Why should I?"

"Don't ask questions, just do it." Kicsi felt an urgency sharp as hunger well up within her. "Please."

"A card. All right." Ilona took a card. "Like this?"

"Yes. Don't let me see it. All right."

"Now what?"

"Now I tell you what card you took."

"Do I get to look at it?"

"Well, of course," said Kicsi. "How else am I going to read your mind?"

"Read my— Oh." Ilona glanced at the card. "All right."

"All right," said Kicsi. "It's—ten of hearts?"

"No."

"No? Wait, let me do it one more time. It's— Is it—"

"This is stupid," said Ilona. The card fluttered to the floor like a wounded white bird. "Really. I think you'd have better things to do with your time. We're leaving soon." She left the room.

Kicsi reached slowly for the card. She remembered a time when she could tell Ilona everything, when they had stayed up talking and giggling until Sarah had had to come and tell them to go to sleep. Now she wondered what had happened, when she had stopped talking to her sister. Perhaps it had been when Vörös came. She felt for pockets for the cards, found none, and started downstairs.

It was dark when the family arrived at the courtyard of the synagogue. The clouds had gone, and the stars in the

sky were as fiery as the eyes of angels. Several people
carried candles and helped the guests to their places, the
men to one side and the women to the other. They heard
murmurs as they passed—surprise that the rabbi had invited Imre and his family. Kicsi found Erzsébet, and they
stood together, not talking, as the ceremony started.

Three violinists started to play. The rabbi's wife and
daughter began to walk to the wedding canopy. The daughter wore a long white gown. She moved carefully through
the crowd; she could not see through her heavy veil.

Kicsi soon lost sight of them. She moved through the
crowd until she could see the canopy. It was supported
by four poles and made of white silk and elaborately em-
broidered with flowers and birds.

The groom and his parents followed the bride to the
canopy. The groom and bride had never met. Years ago,
and following months of negotiations, the rabbi had agreed
to betrothe his daughter to the son of a family from a
nearby town. The two now stood beneath the canopy, before a small table covered with a white cloth. On the table
stood a decanter of wine, two goblets, and a delicate glass
wrapped in white linen.

The music stopped and the rabbi began to speak. Kicsi
grew bored, shifting from one foot to the other. The bride
and groom drank wine from the goblets, the bride lifting
her veil to reach the cup. As the groom placed the ring on
the bride's finger, a woman nearby began to cry softly.

Kicsi looked around. A short round woman was wiping
her eyes with a handkerchief. Her soft blond wig had
been pushed to one side. She took a deep breath, held it,
and began, helplessly, to cry again.

The rabbi lifted the small glass from the table. It was
customary for the groom to crush a glass with his foot as
a reminder of the destruction of the Temple in Jerusalem.
The woman's cries grew louder. The rabbi leaned on his
cane and turned toward the woman's section, annoyed at
the interruption. The glass slipped from the cloth and
shattered on the ground.

A sigh passed through the people of the town like wind.
Folks believed that the groom must crush the glass to
ensure good luck for the marriage. Talk sprang up suddenly. And still the woman cried, her sobs jagged as the
shards of broken glass.

The rabbi looked through the crowd for her. "Tell me," he said. "Why have you disturbed the ceremony? What is making you unhappy?"

The woman had covered her face with her handkerchief and did not realize that the rabbi was talking to her. A sob shuddered through her. She looked up and wiped the tears from her face. "I—I'm sorry. I'm sorry."

The rabbi frowned. "Who are you? Why are you crying?"

"It's—it's because of my son, rabbi. I'm the cousin of the groom's mother. They told me their son was marrying your daughter, and they told me—they said that you—that you could do miracles." This last was almost a question. "And I meant to ask you later about my son, after the wedding, in a few days—" Sobs took hold of her again, and she bowed her head until they released her.

"What has happened to your son? Where is he?"

"I don't know," she said. "I mean, I don't know where he is, if he's alive or dead. I—my husband and I sent him to Germany, to stay with our relatives, and to study there. And, well, and he hasn't answered any of our letters, and we haven't heard from anyone—" She passed her hands across her eyes. "I would have waited until after the wedding, but he—the young bridegroom—he looks so much like our son, and our son would be marrying about now . . ."

"And what do you expect me to do?" asked the rabbi.

"I don't know. To tell me. To tell me if he is alive or dead."

The rabbi sighed. "I can't do that. I don't know. Why should he be dead? He is busy studying. He cannot answer your letters."

"He is dead." Kicsi could not see the speaker, who stood with the men on the other side of the courtyard, but she recognized the voice. It was Vörös. She had not known that he was there. "I am sorry," he said. "All the Jews in Germany are dead, or will be soon."

The woman nodded. She did not cry again. She looked as if she had expected Vörös's answer, as if she could now go on living, no longer so fearfully uncertain.

The rabbi turned to Vörös. "And who are you? What is your business here?"

"I am a traveler."

"Ah. I've heard of you. You call yourself Vörös. You claim to be a magician. They say you destroyed the curse I put on the school."

"I don't—"

"I say you're a cheap conjurer and a liar. You have no business here, at the wedding of my daughter. You're a troublemaker. You had no reason to tell that woman that her son is dead. You know nothing."

"I know that we are living in unsafe times. I know that you—all of you—should flee, should go somewhere safe—Palestine, England, America. You should go now. Soon it will not be safe. You will—"

"Silence!" said the rabbi. Clouds covered the stars and the lights of the candles went out suddenly. The rabbi's face could be seen dimly, pale as tallow. "What are you thinking of, to talk of these evil omens at my daughter's wedding? Get out. You are not welcome in this town."

A sudden intense light blazed upward. Shadows sprang back to the walls of the synagogue. Some of the people holding the candles dropped them in fear. The candles were lit again. Stars pierced the clouds like sword points.

"I will leave now," said Vörös. The townspeople looked at him. The light was not bright, but they stood as though dazzled, blinking like fish on land. "I know what I am saying. Please, all of you. You must leave before it is too late." The clouds curled back slowly, revealing the stars standing like bright shells on the ocean floor.

"If I ever see you here again," said the rabbi, "I will call upon God to strike you dead. Do you understand? You will die, and not by natural means. Your body will wither and your soul will fly forever homeless across the face of the earth. Do you understand?"

"*Sholom aleichem,*" said Vörös.

"The rest of you," the rabbi said. "Don't listen to this foolishness. There is no reason to leave the town. I don't know why this man is trying to frighten you. Nothing will happen to you. Nothing at all."

He looked at the small table. There, wrapped in whitest linen, stood the glass, unbroken. Someone must have gotten a new glass, he thought, though he knew that no one had left the courtyard. He felt old suddenly, the way he had felt the night Vörös had stopped the presses, and sagged forward against his cane. He set the glass on the ground, and the groom, trembling, lifted his heel and crushed it.

"Mazel tov!" said a few of the guests, and—*"Mazel tov!"*—the cry was taken up by others. Some began to clap hands and dance, slowly at first, but soon faster and faster, as if by movement they could forget what had happened. The violinists played a fast, jagged tune. Kicsi did not stay for the dances or for the procession toward the rabbi's house and the feast following the wedding. In the confusion she slipped away to follow Vörös.

"Kicsi!" Erzsébet whispered urgently, "where are you going?" Kicsi shrugged away, moving through the crowd. It was difficult getting to Vörös because he had been with the men and she with the women. Two women blocked her, talking excitedly.

"Did you see what the rabbi did? The glass was unbroken, as good as new. How did he do it?"

"Ah, but how did Vörös light the candles again? That's what I'd like to know."

She walked past them, awkward in her sister's clothes, at last crossing over into the men's section. No one stopped her. She watched the men's faces move past her, rising out of the shadows into the candlelight. Vörös was not among them.

She turned and began to walk away from the synagogue, toward the forest. The streets were deserted, the merrymakers headed in the other direction to the rabbi's house. She looked back once, as if to get her bearings, and saw, far away, the lights of the revelers, dwarfed by the fierce stars above. Their faint cries were blown back to her. Then she was alone.

She began to run. Chimneys and doors, trees and stars were whirled about her like parts of a dream. The pale white road carried her on its back like a swift horse, past the houses, past the town. The gravel-paved road turned to a dirt road, and still she ran on, until she came to the old forest. Then she stopped, breathing heavily. Her mouth was very dry.

She stepped into the forest. The trees were blurred together in the night. They arched high above her, hiding the stars. She could see nothing. She heard leaves rustling softly, endlessly. Slowly she walked forward. A small swift animal ran past her, and she jumped back.

"Who is it? Is anyone there?"

"Vörös!" Her eyes began to grow accustomed to the forest, and she saw him ahead, a dark form sitting on the ground among the fallen leaves and twigs. His long legs were drawn up and his head rested on his knees. He looked as though he were crying. No, Kicsi thought. He would not cry.

A dog, a dark stain against the trees, paced back and forth beside him. As she came farther into the forest the dog drew closer to Vörös, as if protecting him. The dog seemed to stare at her for a long moment, measuring her. Then he turned away.

Kicsi walked up to Vörös and sat down. He looked up at her. "Is that your dog?" she asked.

"Him?" said Vörös. "No, he belongs to no one."

There was silence. Kicsi moved slightly, rustling the broken twigs underfoot. "What will you do now?" she asked.

"Try to save all of you from your own folly," Vörös said. His voice was as bitter as the herbs they ate at Passover. "Though God knows why I should."

"What do you mean?"

"There is one thing more I can do," Vörös said. "I will have to try. Though I will probably fail this time too. I am so tired."

"What will—"

He looked at her directly and she felt warmed, special. "Kicsi. Why aren't you with the others? You shouldn't have come here."

"I—I wanted to talk to you. I missed you. After you left, after the presses stopped. I wanted to tell you that."

"I missed you too, Kicsi. I missed your family. Sometimes I forget what it's like to have a family, the warmth. I need to visit yours, every once in a while."

"Didn't you—were you an orphan?"

He was silent. "I want to thank you," he said at last. "You've reminded me of what it is I am trying to save. Would you mind if I gave you a present?"

"I— Would I mind? No."

"Here," he said. He pulled out a necklace that had lain hidden under his shirt and unlocked the clasp. "Here. Put this on. Perhaps it will protect you. You at least. Who can say? Wear it always."

She held out her hand and he gave her the necklace. From one end dangled a six-pointed star. It shone silver with its own light. Slowly she put it on over her head.

"Here, like this." He showed her how the clasp worked. "Like this. Why are you crying? Kicsi?"

"Because—because you are leaving us again. You're giving me something to make me feel better about it, but you're going to leave, and this time you won't be back."

"Nonsense. I'm not going to leave. I'm right here. I'll be here for quite a while."

"But—you aren't afraid? The rabbi says he will kill you, and your soul—"

"Will fly homeless across the earth. I know. I don't care. I've been traveling homeless for a long time. It shouldn't matter if I do it when I'm dead. Besides," Vörös said, "I don't believe he can kill me."

Kicsi looked up and sniffed softly. She fingered the chain at her neck. "You'll have to tell Father where I got this. Where does it come from?"

"Palestine. It's very old."

"Oh," she said, holding the star. Then: "What did you mean by saving us? Saving us from what?"

"From a man—I see him in my dreams sometimes—"

"A man with no teeth," Kicsi said.

Vörös looked up at her, surprised. "You've seen him too?"

"Once. I saw him in my dream, once. I forgot about it until now. Who is he? He—is he—will he hurt us?"

Vörös shook his head. "I don't know," he said. "God knows. I cannot see all possibilities. It may be as the rabbi says. Nothing at all may happen."

Kicsi felt suddenly cold, alone. Her familiar world was ending, torn into pieces around her. Vörös put his arm around her and held her silently for a few minutes.

"You'd better go now," he said finally. "Your parents will be worrying about you. I don't want to be responsible for you, along with everything else."

She stood up and brushed the dirt and leaves off her dress. "Good-bye," she said. She held the star in her hand one last time. "And thank you. Thank you very much." She tucked the necklace inside the dress, thinking, I'll have enough explaining to do without that. Then she left the forest. The dog saw her go and made a questioning noise deep in its throat.

She walked back slowly. All the houses along the gravel-paved road were dark—all except the rabbi's house, which grew brighter and louder as she drew near it. She opened the door and let herself in.

People were leaving, calling out, "Good-bye! *Mazel tov!*" She edged past them, down the entrance hall, and into the large dining room. The feast was nearly over. A few of the candles set along the tables had gone out, and the rest flickered as the door was opened and closed. Servants were just beginning to clear away the empty plates and cups that lay strewn across the tables like drunks. Several men danced in a circle near the center of the room to a lively tune played by the violinists. Another man sat on the floor and watched them, his hand beating tiredly to the music. Kicsi looked around for her parents.

"Kicsi!" whispered Erzsébet. "Where have you been? What's happened to you? You've got dirt on your dress."

"Please be quiet," said Kicsi. "Where are my parents? Are they worried about me?"

"Over there, with your cousin," said Erzsébet. "I think they thought you were with me the whole evening."

"Good," said Kicsi. "Do you think there's any food left?"

"Kicsi!" said Imre. "We've leaving now."

"Tell me later what happened, all right?" Erzsébet whispered.

"What happened?" said Kicsi. She yawned. "Nothing. I went for a walk, that's all. Good night."

She followed her family out the door. Her eyes closed on the way home and Imre had to carry her the rest of the way. The night wove itself into her dreams.

Chapter

4

Kicsi did not go back to the forest right away. For her it was enough to know that Vörös would be there, that at any time she could go to visit him. She carried the knowledge with her like a secret, like the star she wore near her heart. Meanwhile she talked to no one about Vörös, and the villagers thought that he had gone.

When she did return, a few weeks later, she could not find him. The red and orange leaves had fallen, covering the ground with silent, unmoving fire. The forest was quieter now, whispering softly and slowly like old people remembering their youth. Branches had fallen across the paths or lay snagged in the trees like ancient spiderwebs. For a moment Kicsi feared that Vörös had gone deeper into the forest to where she could not follow him, or that he had left the village. Then from somewhere a dog howled.

Kicsi returned the way she had come, following the sound. The howl came again, closer this time. She saw Vörös and the black dog off in the distance, sitting on a small red hill overlooking the forest, and she ran toward them.

"Hello," she said, sitting beside Vörös. Then, quickly, before he could ask her to leave: "What are you doing?"

"Looking at the earth," said Vörös. "There's fine clay here. Your village has good bones. What brings you out here?"

"I wanted to ask you a question."

"Another question!" Vörös said, laughing.

"Yes," she said. "I wanted to ask— There's a hole in our roof. Did you— I mean, did the rabbi— Do you have anything to do with that?"

"A hole in your roof?"

"Yes. They're fixing it today. That's why I remembered it."

"I had nothing to do with it. What would I want with a hole in your roof? Perhaps a tree—"

"There wasn't any tree nearby," said Kicsi. "I think the rabbi did it."

"The rabbi?" said Vörös gravely. He picked up a stick and turned it over and over without seeing it. "It could be. It could be. But, Kicsi, that's all over now. The curse is gone. There's nothing to worry about."

"Nothing to worry about!" she said, suddenly angry. "He says he will kill you!"

"I told you," said Vörös. "I don't think that he can."

"You don't know him," said Kicsi. "He's—he's— If he wants to kill you, he can do it."

"Ah," said Vörös. "But he does not know me either."

Kicsi sighed. "You haven't grown up here. You don't know. Once, János, the old shoemaker—he disappeared for a while. And his wife went to the rabbi to get him back. And the next day—it was terrible. He came back, bleeding and limping. I heard someone tell my parents that a wolf had chased him back from the next town." Vörös looked at her. He was smiling slightly. "All right, so you don't believe me! You think you've seen wonderful things in your travels, but the rabbi—he really can work miracles. He really does. My father—once he needed an operation—"

"I believe you," said Vörös.

"You—you do?"

"Yes."

"And you're not afraid? Why not?"

44

"I think I can protect myself. I will need time, though, and quiet."

"What will you do?"

"For the moment, nothing. Hush." He sat awhile, studying the ground between his knees.

"Vörös?" said Kicsi a while later.

"Hmmm? Yes?"

"Why don't you ever answer my questions?"

Vörös laughed. He turned her head so that she faced him and looked into her eyes. "A magician's business is with words. He may use other things to help him along—amulets and so forth—but it is within words that the power lies. To choose the wrong words may mean death. And so magicians learn, from the first, to use as few words as possible, to answer as few questions as we can. And that," he said, smiling softly, "may be the longest answer I've ever given you. Now let me be. I must study the land a while longer."

After a long while he stood up. The dog looked up at him.

Vörös began to pace. Then, as though he had come to a decision, he walked a large circle around Kicsi and the spot where he had been sitting. "What do you think?" he said to the dog.

The dog nodded once.

"Good," said Vörös. "Now, Kicsi, once I begin, you may not leave the circle. Do you understand?"

"Did you just talk to the dog? Can he understand you?"

Vörös sighed. "Yes, I did, and yes, he can. If you have to be home, if you have something to do or somewhere to go, you must leave now. If you stay, you cannot leave the circle once I've begun."

"All—all right." She meant to ask him what he planned to do, but something stopped her.

"Good. Now then." He paced the circle again, speaking a few words. Kicsi could tell that they were Hebrew, but the accent was harsher, more angular, than the one she was used to. A thin white line, pale as a scar, sprang up along the ground where he had walked, fencing them in. He returned to the center. The dog continued to prowl the outer edge of the circle.

Vörös sat down. He placed his hands on the ground and began to sing softly, tunelessly. Nothing happened for a long time and Kicsi started to stand up. The air was hot and still. A few grains of sand blew noiselessly along the ground. More joined them, and still more, and suddenly Kicsi saw that they were all moving toward the center of the circle, toward Vörös. She sat back down and put her hand out. There was no breeze. Sand hit her hand sharply, biting like bitter cold, and she pulled her hand back. Vörös continued to sing.

The grains of sand flowed together, thickened, became clay. The clay grew under Vörös's hands. As he sang he pulled it from the ground, forming it, shaping it, giving it texture, calling it to him. Red rivers grew at his feet, humping out of the ground, flowing into pools. He stood.

The pools grew slowly. Wet clay touched the hem of Kicsi's dress and she moved away, toward the edge. Beyond the circle everything looked shapeless and pale. The forest, the paths, the sun wavered as though they were woven into a tapestry hanging in the wind. She walked closer to the white line, trying to see. The dog turned to her and growled low in its throat, rumbling like a distant train. Vörös looked at her and she sat down quickly.

Vörös raised his hands and began another song, this one fast and full of melody. Air brushed past Kicsi's cheek, moving toward his hands. The wind grew stronger, quicker, spinning about Vörös, tossing his clothes, his hair. The wind howled like mourners. Vörös stood steadily, his mouth opening and closing in the words of the song, but he could not be heard.

The clay spun around the whirlwind. Higher and higher it rose, spinning itself out like rope, until it had grown past the tops of the trees. Vörös stopped the wind then, letting his hands fall to his sides, and the clay fell slowly to earth, folding back upon itself in layers. The clay stood still, an unformed shape in the middle of the circle.

Vörös sang softly, coaxingly, to the clay, like a mother singing to her child. The clay began to shape itself, to flow, to change its outlines. It formed for itself a head, an arm, a leg.

Suddenly Kicsi saw that all Vörös's magic was based on illusion. With his song he sought to beguile the clay into thinking it was a man. He sang to it of man-things: of hard work and sleep, of sun and rain, snow and mist, of comfort and pain. Come away, he sang. Be clay no more. Be a man.

The clay took one slow step toward Vörös. Then it toppled forward slowly, falling with no sound. One of its legs lay twisted under it at an impossible angle.

Vörös bent over the clay form. He straightened the leg, smoothed out the damage it had suffered in the fall. Then he sat back, staring off at the forest. The protective white line had disappeared and everything outside the circle was as clear as before.

"What is it?" said Kicsi. "Is it a golem?"

Vörös looked at her sharply. He seemed surprised that she was still there. "Yes," he said. His voice was hoarse.

"I've heard stories about golems," Kicsi said, "Erzsébet's father tells them. There was a rabbi somewhere in Prague —I forget his name—who made a golem to protect the people. He was alive, but he couldn't talk. The golem, I mean. Is that what you were trying to do?" She paused, looked at the still clay form. "Why didn't it work?"

"It needs more words," said Vörös.

"What do you mean?"

"More words," Vörös repeated, as if he thought that Kicsi had not heard him.

"I don't—I don't understand." She looked at him. He was very white; against his pale skin his scar gleamed like a sword. His blue eyes were large and expressionless. "Oh. You're tired. I'm sorry. I'll go home now."

"Yes," said Vörös. "Please."

"Can I—can I come back tomorrow?"

Vörös nodded.

"All right. Good-bye." She walked away slowly, stopped, and turned around. Vörös had slumped against the golem, his eyes closed. "Good-bye," she said softly.

It was late when she finally came home. The family had started supper. "Kicsi," said Sarah. "There you are. You've gotten stains all over your dress. How on earth did you manage that? Where have you been? Erzsébet's mother told me she'd seen you going to the forest."

Kicsi said nothing. She slipped quietly into her place at the table.

"Maybe she's got a boyfriend," said Magda.

"Don't be silly," said Kicsi.

"Kicsi's got a boyfriend," said Ilona. "Kicsi's got—"

"Be quiet!" said Kicsi.

"Yes, please," said Imre. "Kicsi, have you been to the forest? I'm sure your mother needs you at home. And are you doing your schoolwork?"

"Of course," said Kicsi, thinking about that day's assignment that she had not done yet.

"I don't want you out neglecting your studies," said Sarah. "Your father practically risked his life—we all did—so that you children could go to that school."

"I know," said Kicsi.

"And I don't like you going to that forest," said Sarah. "There are—things—in that forest. It isn't safe. Your great-uncle saw his dead wife's ghost there once. And there are animals there, too. Wolves."

"I'm very careful," said Kicsi. "And I leave when it starts getting dark. You don't have to worry."

"All right," said Sarah. "But I don't like it. I wish you'd find someplace else to go. And tomorrow, I want you right here after school, so I can see you doing your schoolwork. Then you can go off to the forest."

"But—but I can't—"

"Why? What else do you have to do?"

I can't tell you, Kicsi thought. I want to tell you about Vörös, and the clay, and the dog, but you won't believe me. Or you'll forbid me to go. And it might get back to the rabbi that Vörös hasn't left yet, and he might be—might be— No, I can't tell anyone.

"Nothing," she said aloud. "I'll be here. You'll see."

She hurried through her schoolwork the next day and ran straight to the forest after she was done, but still she was late getting there. Evening was near, and the day was growing cold. Vörös and the dog had already started marking out the circle. She sat a small distance away, behind a rock, out of sight of any prying eyes from the village.

Suddenly the dog stopped. He pointed his head toward the forest. His ears lay flat and he growled, showing his teeth. Vörös looked around and Kicsi, after a while, did the same. There, picking his way slowly through the trail that led from the forest, making no sound, was the rabbi.

He came to the hill and stopped, leaning on his cane. Then he began to walk again. He climbed the hill with difficulty and stopped every so often, but still he came on.

He made no sound as he walked over the leaves and sand and rocks, and Kicsi shivered. Vörös did not move.

"Good day to you, traveler," said the rabbi. He thrust his cane through the protective circle and the white line snapped apart with the sound of sparks crackling. The cane was still raised as he walked across the circle and sat down on a small rock. Then he balanced his cane against his knees, lifted his hat, and adjusted the skullcap beneath it, never once looking away from Vörös.

"Good day," said Vörös calmly, still standing. He looked around at the dog, who stood motionless, and at Kicsi, still well hidden behind the rock.

"I suppose it can be argued," said the rabbi, "whether this hill is indeed part of the town. During the Sabbath, when one is not supposed to travel farther than the limits of the town, it is true that no one comes here. And if this hill is not part of the town then I suppose you are safe, for I said that I would kill you if I ever saw you in the town again."

"I suppose so," said Vörös.

"Still," said the rabbi, "it may be that you will go into the town again—to get food, supplies, whatever you need. And if you do—if you bother us again—I will be waiting."

"Yes," said Vörös.

"Don't be so calm!" said the rabbi. "Do you suppose that I want to kill you? I wish I had never seen you. Every day I watch my daughter, to see if all is well with her, and every day I give thanks to God that she is healthy and happy. But if she dies, if she dies, you are responsible for her death just as surely as if you killed her, because yours were the words of evil omen spoken at the wedding. I don't want to kill you. I just want you to leave us alone. I want you to go back to your home, if you have a home, or to wherever it is you came from. You have caused enough trouble in this town."

"I have things that I must do here."

"Well, then, you have been warned. I have warned you what will happen if you continue to meddle in the affairs of this town."

"I'm not afraid of you."

"No?" The rabbi's bushy eyebrows moved closer together. "Well, then. We shall see. I suppose you think that your knowledge of sorcery is greater than mine. It is true that you removed the curse that I set on Imre's household, but that was only a very minor piece of spell-work. I was not expecting someone like you to happen along."

"I go where I must."

"Hmmm?" said the rabbi. He raised his eyebrows and looked at Vörös with clear, expressionless gray eyes. "Perhaps there are other forces at work here. I was not expecting that. Perhaps you work for the devil? Hmmm?"

"You know that isn't true."

"No. Well. You're just a troublemaker, as I first suspected. Perhaps you think you can win against me because you broke my spell of darkness at the wedding. Again, that was a very minor thing. I was testing your power."

"I knew you were," said Vörös. "Though you have never thanked me for making the cup whole again."

"Did you do that? No. I know you didn't do that. I don't know why, but you want to destroy us—my family, my daughter. Someone got another cup for us."

"Very well then. Think what you please about me. But you know that no one left the courtyard."

"No," said the rabbi. He was almost speaking to himself. "You want to destroy us. I don't know why. I don't know who sent you. But I must destroy you first." He looked up at Vörös and spoke louder. "Ah, but you have one advantage. You know my name, traveler, and I do not know yours."

"I am called Vörös."

The rabbi laughed. "You know better than that! You have survived many years, sorcerer—and I sense that you are old, older than you look—and so you must at least know the importance of names. With the proper names one can control all the angels of heaven and the demons of hell. It is said that the prophet Elijah knew seventeen of the names of the demoness Lilith, the child-stealer, and so kept her away from houses with newborns."

Vörös said nothing.

"So, then, what is your name?" the rabbi went on. "There should be some way to discover it. Let's see. You say your name is Vörös, and Vörös means red. Red is *adom* in Hebrew. Our father Adam was so called because he was made from the red earth—earth much like this." He spread his hand over the red clay. "So perhaps you are Adam? But no, it says in the first book of the Torah that

Adam, though he lived a long life, finally died, like all men. So you cannot be Adam. But we shall see. I will discover your true name sooner or later. I do not like to be at a disadvantage."

Vörös smiled. "Perhaps you will," he said.

"Perhaps!" said the rabbi. "You underestimate me, traveler. You say you are not frightened of me. Then yield up your true name to me now. It should be nothing for one such as you, who has no fear."

"I am not a fool," said Vörös, still smiling.

"No," said the rabbi. "I thought not. I do believe I could destroy you if I knew your true name."

"I don't want it to come to that between us," said Vörös.

"No? Good. Then stay out of my village and away from my people. And one other thing. I hear from the villagers that you have been spending your time with Imre's youngest daughter."

The rabbi looked around the hill, taking in everything with his wide gray eyes. Kicsi hunched further behind the rock.

"Kicsi?" said Vörös.

"Yes, that's the one. I don't want you to see her again. You're a bad influence on her. I don't want her exposed to the black sorcery, especially at so young an age."

Vörös smiled. "I am not a black sorcerer."

"So you say. Keep away from her. I am not the only one concerned about her. Her father, too, is worried."

"He has nothing to worry about."

"I hope you are right," said the rabbi. "I must go now. And again I warn you. If I find you in the village again, I will kill you."

"Good day," said Vörös.

The rabbi stood and walked slowly down the hillside. The dog, who had stood motionless during the exchange between Vörös and the rabbi, began to twitch as though released from a spell. He watched the rabbi as he faded into the evening. Then he whined, and looked at Vörös.

"It's all right," said Vörös. "He has not said anything I did not know."

"Vörös!" said Kicsi. She ran out from behind the rock and hugged him, holding on to him tightly. "Vörös, he is going to kill you! And what will he do to me, if he finds me here with you? Is he going to kill me too? I'm frightened, Vörös, I'm so frightened."

"Don't worry," said Vörös soothingly. "I've told you not to worry. He won't harm you."

"Why is he so angry with you? You didn't—you didn't do what he says, did you? Curse his daughter?"

"No. No, he is angry with me because I see something he does not see, or has seen and forgotten."

Kicsi stepped away from him. "Can I come back tomorrow?"

Vörös laughed. "I thought you were frightened."

"I—I am. But I want to see what will happen. Can I come back?"

"How do you know that anything will happen?"

"Oh." She paused. "I don't—I guess I don't really know. Will the rabbi be back?"

"I think so."

"Can I watch?"

"All right," said Vörös. "But stay behind the rock again, exactly as you did today. That was a very wise thing you did, when you did not move from the rock."

She smiled at his praise. "I was too frightened to move," she said.

He laughed. "All right then. I'll see you tomorrow."

Kicsi looked around her. In the twilight the golem was no more than another stone. "Why didn't he see the golem?"

"The protection on the circle still extended that far," said Vörös. "There was a spell on him so that he was unable to see it. But I think," he said, looking toward the setting sun, "that I shall let him see it tomorrow. It will not hurt to let him know what I have in mind."

"I'd better go now," said Kicsi. "It's very late."

"Yes," said Vörös. "Good-bye." He called after her as she ran down the hillside. "And good luck!"

The rabbi arrived the next day, shortly after Kicsi had taken her place behind the rock. Vörös had not put up the protective circle, and so the rabbi found him bent over the still clay form.

"Ah," said the rabbi, seating himself on a rock. "So you are making a golem."

Vörös said nothing.

"It is interesting that you should attempt that," said the

rabbi. "It has not been done successfully since fifteen-eighty, as far as I know. Yet you think you will succeed, of course, or you would not have gone to the trouble. May I ask what you are making him for?"

Vörös looked up. He was very pale; even his eyes seemed to have lost color. Kicsi thought, shocked, that he looked as though he had not slept all night. Perhaps he had given the golem more words, as he said he would. "To protect the village," he said.

"I protect the village, not you," the rabbi said emphatically. "Do you think the people here do not know that? I am their teacher, their adviser, their"—he looked to the golem again, and his voice, though lowered, carried to where Kicsi sat concealed by the rock—"magician. We do not need you here among us to create trouble. I am afraid you see monsters where none exist."

"I see a man in my dreams," said Vörös. "I see him often. A man with no teeth."

The rabbi looked up, startled.

"Ah," said Vörös, "you see him too."

"So what if I do? They are dreams, nothing more."

"No, rabbi," Vörös said. "They are not just dreams. You know what they are. Please, tell the people they are not safe here. They listen to you, not to me."

"They listen to me," the rabbi said. "They listen because I have never advised them wrongly. What will they say if I suddenly tell them to leave their homes, their synagogue, their village—all on the strength of a dream?"

Vörös looked at him. Light broke against his eyes and he looked as though he were seeing some terror. "Rabbi," he said levelly, "they will thank you."

The rabbi shrugged. "I have lived here longer than you," he said. "I know my people, and you do not." He bent over and peered at the golem.

"I see you have nothing written on the golem's forehead," the rabbi said. "I know that you understand the importance of names. I am curious. Tell me. There are many schools of thought concerning the word that should be written on the forehead of a golem. Which word will you choose?"

"I do only as I have been taught," said Vörös.

"Ah! And who taught you? That would be an interesting thing to learn. There are those who teach that the Holy

Name of God should be written on the golem's forehead to bring him to life and that to take away the gift of life one must erase the Name." The rabbi paused. Vörös said nothing. "And then there are those who believe that the word *emes*, truth, should be the word written on the forehead, and that to take away life one must erase the first letter, the *aleph*, so that the word on his forehead is now the word for death.

"Ah, so you will not speak," said the rabbi. "Very well then. I shall be back tomorrow to see the progress you have made. *Sholom aleichem.*"

The rabbi stood and began to walk down the hill. Vörös spoke softly to the golem, swaying back and forth, his words falling like rain falling on bare ground. The rabbi turned back, puzzled.

"You are a very rude man," he said. "I trust we will be rid of you soon."

Vörös stopped the flow of his words. He picked up a sharpened stick from the ground and wrote a word on the golem's forehead. Then he moved back so that the rabbi could read the word he had written. It was Adam.

"That is blasphemy!" said the rabbi. "You are not God. You cannot play like this with creation!"

The rabbi stepped back. His eyes were bright with rage. He lifted his cane and pointed it at Vörös.

For a moment nothing happened. Then the world exploded. The forest tore free of the sky and the sun skittered away like a top. Kicsi held on tightly to the rock and closed her eyes. A noise filled the world, drowning it in thunder, and went on and on forever. She lived alone in an agony of darkness and sound. She opened her eyes.

Vörös lay on the ground, not moving. The golem got up, slowly, forcing itself to its knees, its feet. It walked unsteadily across the moving ground toward the rabbi.

The rabbi stepped back once more. A look of horror was on his face and he lost control of his spell. The world slowly fit itself together again. He took one step more, then drew himself up and faced the golem. He held up his cane, pointed it at the golem. Suddenly everything stood out sharply in a great flash of light. The earth tossed once more.

The golem's hand rose slowly and covered his forehead and fell down, lifeless. The rabbi's fire had erased the first

54

letter of its name. The word on its forehead now spelled *dam,* blood.

Blood spilled slowly from its wound, blood that could barely be seen against the red of the clay. More blood came, and more, spilling over the golem's arms and legs and on to the ground. The golem wavered. It fell.

Vörös stood. He held his left hand to his forehead, as though he had been hit in the same place as the golem. With his right hand he held tightly to the sharpened stick. He shouted and flung the stick at the rabbi. The ground burst into flames at the rabbi's feet.

The rabbi stepped back. He passed his cane over the flames and they fell away. Then he moved forward, his face twisted into a smile.

"It may be that I will not need your name to defeat you, eh, traveler?"

"It may be," said Vörös, breathing heavily. Blood dripped from his forehead into his eyes, and he wiped them with his sleeve.

"You put a lot of yourself into the golem, did you not, traveler?" said the rabbi.

"You know I did," said Vörös.

The rabbi came on. "I am fond of my daughter, too, traveler."

"Rabbi," said Vörös. He swallowed. "Then we are even, you and I. More than even, for your daughter lives and my creation is dead." He pointed to the golem. It could now barely be distinguished from the earth.

The rabbi laughed. "But I love my daughter. What do you know of love, traveler? Did you love your golem? I do not think so."

The rabbi raised his cane again. Once again the earth was forced apart. Boulders ran down the hillside. Trees fell crashing to the forest floor.

Vörös raised his hands. With an obvious effort he calmed the trees, the hill.

The rabbi came forward. "You are weakening, are you not, sorcerer?"

Vörös moved back. He stumbled over a stone and was down so suddenly that Kicsi had not seen it happen. The rabbi stood over him.

"Is it true that you think that you are God?" said the rabbi.

"No," said Vörös.

"Once you said you were not afraid," said the rabbi. "What do you say now?"

"I am still not afraid," said Vörös. He tried to stand, but could not. "Kill me now."

The dog moved suddenly. He grew as hazy as fire smoke. In his place stood a tall man in a long robe and brightly colored cap.

"Who—who are you?" said the rabbi. His eyes moved from Vörös to the man.

"I am called Akan," said the man. His voice was very deep. "You will not have heard my real name."

"That does not matter to me," said the rabbi. He raised his cane a third time. "Your friend lies bound and helpless. In a few minutes he will be dead."

"No!" said Akan. He raised his hands. Flames leapt up in a circle around the rabbi, hemming him in. Closer and closer they came to him. Kicsi thought she saw his long coat catch fire.

The rabbi twisted like a bird caught in a cage. Through the red walls of fire Kicsi could see him raise and lower his cane. She could feel the heat of the fire.

He cried out one long, despairing word and turned and threw his cane through the fire at Akan. The other man screamed and clutched his head. Then he was gone. The flames went out.

The rabbi stood awhile, trying to catch his breath. Then he said, "Ah, that was intended for your friend Vörös." He turned back to where Vörös had fallen, but Vörös was not there. He laughed softly. "So, you have escaped me once again. No, I am not angry. I only hope that you do not come back. I hope that we have seen the last of you." He bent down and picked up his cane. It was barely singed.

He walked with difficulty, leaning on his cane, to where Akan had last stood. "Your friend was better at withstanding me, I see. I did not mean for this to happen. Him I would have taken apart piece by piece and thrown to the winds, as I did you. But I did not bear a grudge against you. You I did not know."

The rabbi stood straighter and held heavily to his cane. "But," he said, "if you had any part in this blasphemy, if you sought in any way to take upon yourself the function of the Creator, then I have done well. Then I have made no mistake. And of course, if you were a friend of the traveler, then you had probably meddled too far in the black sorcery for the good of your soul."

He poked with his cane at the remains of the golem. "Ah, that is something I would like to know." Then he shivered, and wrapped his torn coat tighter around him. Twilight had come upon them during the battle. "But it is probably for the best that I never find out."

He turned and walked down the hill, making no sound.

Kicsi came out from behind the rock. She could still hear faintly the terrible sound of the world being torn down the middle, sounding in her mind like a distant bell ringing forever. She began to shiver violently and sat down for a long time until she could walk. Far off, she heard howls and shrieks—animals crying in the forest—and she looked up. A few trees were on fire, and the blaze caught quickly.

She stood up, holding to the rock for support. It was as if nothing had happened. Vörös and the rabbi were gone, Akan was dead, and the golem was as if it had never been. She could not even see any footprints. She could see only the rocks, the red clay, and the paths leading to the forest.

She waited until she was sure the rabbi had left, then began to walk down the hillside. As she went, she tripped over something soft in the dark and she bent down to feel its outlines. It was Vörös's knapsack.

She picked it up—it was surprisingly light—and carried it with her into the town. By the light of the first lamp post she knelt and opened it.

There was a peacock's feather, a fox's tail, pieces of amber, bits of jewelry. There were amulets of gold, of brass, of copper. There were keys attached to a necklace of silver. There were seashells, stones, dried flowers, cloth bags with various sweet-smelling herbs. There were shirts and pants and headgear, but none of a fashion she had ever seen. And finally, at the bottom, there was a small leather bag tied round with ribbons.

She lifted the bag out of the sack and held it in her hands. Then suddenly she was confused. What was she doing? The street seemed to tilt and the lights ran together. She placed the bag back where she had found it in the knapsack and shook her head. She took a deep breath, decided that she felt better, and set off down the street.

When she got home, she went around the side way, lifting the latch on the gate to get into the backyard. With some recently chopped wood she found in the woodpile she dug a hole and put in the sack. Then she covered the sack as neatly as she could and marked the spot with a small piece of wood. Later she would return and hide the sack away in one of the thick walls of the house.

It was only when she opened the front door that she realized it must be very late. The food set on the table had grown cold and everyone stood near the door, waiting. Ilona was crying. Sarah was sitting down and holding her head in her hands. She did not look up as the door opened.

"Kicsi!" said Imre. "Where have you been?" Without waiting for an answer he grasped the back of her neck and walked her forcefully to the window. She could see small flames in the distance, like demons dancing. "Do you see that? The forest is burning. Didn't your mother and I warn you?"

Sarah looked up. "Your dress! Imre, look what she's done to herself. Her dress is ruined! And what happened to your hair?"

Kicsi reached up and touched her short brown hair. It was woven with sand and clay and small rocks.

"Where have you been? Have you been to the forest?"

"Y—Yes."

"What happened to you?"

"The fire—there was a terrible fire—"

"Did you see the fire?" asked Tibor. The others stared at her. "How did it start?"

"I don't know—I don't know."

"All right," said Imre. "That's enough. Kicsi, I forbid you to go to the forest again. Do you hear me?"

She nodded.

"And you may not come and eat with us until you have washed yourself—*and* your hair—and put on clean clothes. And as for the rest of you, you are not to talk about this unless Kicsi shows that she is willing to listen." He pulled her closer to him. "It's all right, Kicsi, it's all right. You can cry now if you want to." But she could not cry.

Later, as she was taking her bath, she realized two

things. The first was that Vörös had escaped the rabbi and was still alive. The second, following the first so closely that she did not have time to feel joy, was a certainty that went deeper than the need for proof. She knew that Vörös would never sit and eat with them again. And then she began to cry.

Chapter

5

A small fine rain had started the morning of Thursday, market day, and had not let up by afternoon. Sarah looked out the windows and stood watching for a moment, then she said, "Let's go, Kicsi. I don't think the rain will keep anyone away."

Sarah picked up her coat and purse. Kicsi put away her schoolbooks and followed Sarah out the door and down toward the crossroads, where the market was set up.

"Now, don't forget—we're having company tomorrow. I'll have to get a large chicken, and—let me see—vegetables—"

Kicsi said nothing. Sarah glanced at her, worried. Kicsi seemed to act much as she always had. She was very often loud and forceful just to make herself heard over the other three children. Sometimes Sarah would hear her say wildly untrue things, and she would have to remind herself that her daughter just wanted to be noticed. Now Sarah sensed that something had happened to Kicsi, that she was troubled and unhappy. More and more Sarah felt that she did not know her daughter at all, and she wondered how much of Kicsi's unhappiness was because of Vörös. She had talked to Imre, but Imre would only say that Kicsi was growing up. Still, all the while she planned dinner a part of Sarah's mind was on her daughter.

A large old truck, its once-green paint peeling, shifted noisily into second gear behind them. Sarah and Kicsi moved quickly to the side of the road. The truck rumbled past them, and they followed it to the marketplace.

The driver got out by one of the stalls and opened one of the rusty rear doors. Sarah recognized him as Sholom, the fish peddler. "Hello, Sholom," she said. "What's new?"

He shrugged, lifting one of the heavy crates out of the truck. "Nothing new." He set the crate down by his stall and wiped the rain from his eyes. "Rain's driven everyone away," he said.

"And Jansci? How's your son?"

Sholom shrugged again. "The same. Me, I sometimes think, if he dies, it will be God's will. But my wife—she's frantic. She's been to see the rabbi every day this week."

"What does the rabbi say?" said Sarah. Kicsi looked up.

"Nothing. What can he say? He prays for him."

Sarah sighed. "It's a terrible thing," she said. "Well, we've got to get going. Come on, Kicsi."

They moved through the marketplace, stopping to chat and to buy a chicken, eggs, some fresh vegetables. The rain was ending as they passed Sholom's stall on their way home. Sholom's wife stood there. "Hello, Perl," said Sarah.

"Hello," said Perl. She fidgeted, twisting her wedding ring on her finger. She turned to her husband. "I've been to see the rabbi again," she said.

"Well," said Sholom. "What does he say?"

"I don't know," said Perl. "He seems—I don't know. Unwilling to talk to me. As though he's thinking of something else."

"Ah," said Sholom. "Thinking of his daughter, I'll bet."

"His daughter?" said Perl.

"You remember, at the wedding. That traveling man, the redhead. He said something—I don't remember what. The rabbi thinks he's cursed his daughter."

"Vörös," said Perl. Her fingers stilled. She stood silently for a moment. "He's a magician, isn't he?" She turned to Sarah. "You knew him, didn't you? He stayed at your house."

Without thinking, Kicsi put her hand to the star she wore under her dress. Perl's eyes moved to her, quick as lightning. "What's that?" she said. "He gave you something? What is it?"

"Show her, Kicsi," said Sarah. "Maybe your charm can help poor Jansci."

Kicsi began to draw out her necklace. She was curiously unwilling. "A charm?" said Perl. "Let me see."

Kicsi held the star in her hand. It shone with a pale silver light. "Let me see it," said Perl. She held out her hand impatiently.

"It's just a necklace," said Kicsi. "It isn't magic. It can't help you." She let the star fall against her dress.

"Kicsi!" said Sarah. "Don't be selfish. Show her the charm. How can you refuse to help them?"

"It's mine," said Kicsi. "Vörös gave it to me." Where is he? she wondered, not for the first time. Is he in danger while I stay here, safe and among friends?

Perl reached for the necklace, held it in her hand. "Please!" she said. Without realizing it she began to pull the star toward her. The chain cut deep into Kicsi's neck. "You have to help us."

"Wait a minute—you're hurting me—" said Kicsi.

"Perl, stop that!" said Sholom. "I'm sure she'll let you borrow the necklace. You have to explain to her—" He could not go on.

"Their son is very sick, Kicsi," said Sarah. "We're afraid that—God forbid—he might die."

"All—all right," said Kicsi finally. "But you can't take the necklace. I'll have to be there when you use it."

"Thank you," said Perl softly. She dropped her hand.

"But anyway, it won't work," said Kicsi. "It's just a necklace."

"Kicsi!" said Sarah. "Don't say such things. You don't know."

"Be at our house tomorrow, after school," said Perl. "Please."

"We will," said Sarah. She embraced Perl awkwardly, holding bags full of food.

They walked along the gravel roads toward home. "Kicsi!" someone called. Kicsi turned. It was Erzsébet, with her mother and someone she did not know.

Sarah and Kicsi slowed. "Hello," said Erzsébet. "This is my cousin, Aladár." She turned to the young man beside her. "Ali, this is my best friend, Kicsi."

"Hello," said Aladár. His voice was pleasant. "What just happened with you and that woman?" He laughed. "She looked like she wanted your head."

Kicsi laughed. "She almost did."

"Ali's going to go to college soon," said Erzsébet. "Tell her about it, Ali. What you told me."

Aladár looked at Kicsi, and, quite suddenly, they both decided not to answer Erzsébet.

"She wanted my necklace," said Kicsi.

"Your necklace?"

"Yes," said Kicsi. "See?" She showed him the star. In the afternoon shadows it shone like a seashell.

"Where did you get that?" said Aladár.

"From Vörös."

"The magician?" said Aladár. Erzsébet shrugged and moved ahead to join her mother and Sarah. Aladár and Kicsi fell behind. "Erzsi told me."

"About Vörös?" Aladár nodded. "They thought it was a magic charm. They wanted to use it to cure their son, Jansci. He's very sick. But I don't think it's a charm at all. I didn't want to give it to them. I thought I was just being selfish—that's what my mother thought, too—but now I don't think so. I think I knew, somehow, that my necklace won't help. I don't want to raise their hopes. Do you know what I mean?"

Aladár nodded. "But you could have been more tactful."

"I know. I have problems with tact. Everyone tells me. I don't know what I could have done though."

"Did you know Vörös?"

"I guess so. As much as anyone here knew him."

"Were you there—at the wedding, I mean?"

"Yes."

"Did you—Say—" He broke off, became thoughtful. Then he said, "Did he teach you anything? You know—sorcery?"

"He showed me how to make a golem once."

"A golem! How?"

She stopped. She had not meant to say that. It was her secret, all that was left to her of Vörös except the star. "I can't tell you."

"Oh, come on! A golem! Did it really move? How did it work?" His friendly round face shone with curiosity.

"I can't tell you. I don't want to."

"I don't believe you. You made it all up."

"No, I didn't! I just don't want to tell you. It was between Vörös and me. No one else knows." Except the rabbi, she thought. "I can't tell you."

"Oh," he said. His brown eyes gleamed. "Well, think about it—"

"Ali!" said Erzsébet. "Ali, we're home! Come on!"

"Think about it and maybe you can tell me tomorrow. Oh, no." He stopped, stricken. "No, I leave tomorrow—"

"Ali!"

"Just a minute! Let me think. Passover. I'll be back for Passover, at Erzsi's house. Tell me then."

"I can't—"

"Good-bye!" he called, and followed Erzsébet. Kicsi watched him go.

The next day Kicsi went with Sarah to Sholom's house.

"Hello," said Perl, subdued now by the nearness of death. "Please, please come in." Sholom stood by the door, smiling shyly. He shrugged. He did not have words for this situation.

"This way," Perl went on. "Over here. Here's his room."

They followed her. János lay on his bed, asleep. His face was furrowed with pain.

"What—what do we do now?" said Kicsi. She was whispering.

"I'm not really sure," said Perl. "Maybe—maybe take out the necklace and hold it over him."

Kicsi undid the clasp. With a sudden movement she lifted the sleeping boy's pillow and placed the star underneath. János moaned softly.

"There. Let him sleep on that overnight," she said.

"I don't—I don't know what to say," Sholom said suddenly. "Thank you. Thank you very much. You are—I think you are some sort of witch yourself. Look at her eyes," he said to Sarah. "She has been touched by magic." He stopped, embarrassed at having said so much. "Do you think—do you think it will work?"

"I don't know," said Kicsi. *"Gut Shabbos."*

"Gut Shabbos," said Sholom. They left him looking at the child.

Sarah had invited Erzsébet and her family to the Sabbath dinner. As they sat down, Erzsébet said, "What did you think of my cousin?"

"Aladár?" said Kicsi. "He seemed very nice. He's going to school now, isn't he?"

"To college."

"How old is he?"

"Sixteen, I think."

"Well," said Kicsi. "I'm fourteen." Suddenly she remembered the rabbi speaking to Vörös: ". . . and I sense that you are old, older than you look."

"You are not—you're thirteen, same as I am."

"I'm almost fourteen."

"Oh," said Erzsébet, laughing. "*Almost* fourteen."

They began to laugh and could not stop. "Did you like him?" said Erzsébet.

"Yes," said Kicsi. She hoped Erzsébet would say more about him. It was much easier for her to talk about Aladár than it was to talk about Vörös. She wondered how old Vörös really was and why she had never told anyone about him and the rabbi. Magicians, she decided, deal too much in secrecy and silence. She would have no more secrets. "Yes, I like him very much. When will he come back? He said something . . ."

"Next Passover," said Erzsébet, eating her chicken. "He'll be spending Passover with us, because his parents live so far from the college. I think he likes you too."

The days passed slowly. Kicsi thought of Vörös and the rabbi. She thought of how she would tell Aladár about the golem. She rehearsed the story to herself, often, as she walked to and from school.

The first snow came and with it the news that Magda was going to marry and live with her husband in a nearby village. The wedding was large, and the villagers attended mostly, Kicsi thought, because of the family's connection with magic. But nothing happened at the wedding—the glass remained unbroken until the groom broke it himself.

Sholom's son János died in the middle of winter. Kicsi could not say why she went to the funeral, but she felt that she had to. The ground in the graveyard had frozen, and the iron shovels of the grave diggers bent before they broke through. Afterward Sholom came up to her and thanked her, haltingly, for coming. "It wasn't your fault," he said, over and over. Silver tears shone in his eyes. "Thank you. You did what you could. It wasn't your fault."

Days passed. Houses stood free of the snow, emerging

as slowly after the winter as the new leaves on the trees. Rain came and washed the snow down the streets. With the spring came Passover. Kicsi began to watch the roads.

Her first surprise came when he drove up in a car. She knew very few people who owned cars, or drove in them. Some students passing through let him off at Erzsébet's house, honking the horn loudly. Erzsébet's family ran outside, gathering around him.

Her second surprise was that he remembered her. "Kicsi!" he said when he saw her standing by the house. She had followed the car to Erzsébet's house. "Hello! Have you decided to tell me that story yet?" Erzsébet's family surrounded him, hugging him, taking his luggage. They pulled him into the house.

"Yes!" she called after him as he waved to her. He was laughing, protesting feebly against Erzsébet's parents. "Tomorrow!"

He was waiting for her in front of Erzsébet's house the next day. They walked to the forest and she showed him the clay the golem had been made of and the charred wood where the forest had caught fire. Clumps of mushrooms grew where the trees had stood.

"Are you sure—I don't mean to doubt your sanity, really—but are you sure you saw what you think you did?" said Aladár. "It's a little hard to believe."

"Of course I'm sure," said Kicsi, plucking at the mushrooms. "I still have his knapsack. There wasn't time for him to take it when he left."

"His knapsack? So he intends to come back."

"I hope so," said Kicsi, standing. "Come on home with me. I'll show you where I keep it."

When they reached the house Kicsi led him to the corridor near the pantry. She pulled loose a few bricks and reached inside the wall. "No one knows it's here," she said, taking out the sack. The gray cat came alongside them, sniffing at the hole in the wall. "Look."

Aladár opened the sack, looked carefully at the charms and herbs. His fingers came finally to the small pouch at the bottom. "I wonder what's in here," he said.

"Don't—"

He started to take out the pouch. His face went blank, and very white. He replaced the pouch slowly. "I don't think I'll try that again," he said, trying to laugh.

"No," said Kicsi.

"Do you know what's in it?"

"No," she said. "I can't take it out either."

"Well then," he said. "Maybe everything you've told me is true."

"Of *course*—" she said, but broke off when she saw his smile.

"I know," he said.

"It's funny," she said. "You're the first person I've told. I didn't think anyone would believe me, but somehow I knew you would. I knew you wouldn't laugh."

"You didn't want to tell me, either," said Aladár. "I think you enjoyed keeping your secret."

"I learned that from Vörös. He was very secretive. Or maybe"—she frowned as a new thought came to her—"maybe I just never knew the right questions to ask. Magicians," she went on—and felt gratified to see that Aladár's eyes were wide with interest—"magicians, you know, never say much about themselves. It's too dangerous."

"And are you like that? Are you secretive?"

"Nooo," she said slowly. The cat curled itself up by the knapsack. "No, not usually. I think—somehow—that Vörös bound me to silence."

"Well, then," said Aladár. "Tell me about yourself. You know, when Erzsi told me that she had a friend named Little One I expected—I don't know—I expected you to be very small, maybe a dwarf." He laughed. "But you're almost as tall as your sisters."

"I know. They've always called me that, though. I've always been the smallest one in the family."

"Doesn't it ever bother you?"

"No, not that. That doesn't bother me. It's—being the youngest, and having to wear all the old hand-me-downs, and being forgotten, and having my parents call me by someone else's name . . ."

"I wouldn't know," said Aladár. "I'm an only child."

"An only—" Kicsi stopped. "I can't imagine that. It sounds wonderful."

"Really? And I thought your family was wonderful. There's always someone around to talk to—"

"Too many people, usually. There's never any privacy. I'm surprised no one's interrupted us yet."

"There's too much privacy in my family. My parents

are very—distant. I can't talk to them. Finally I decided I just had to go away, go to college."

"What's it like, college? What do you study? Do you—"

"Kicsi!" someone called.

"See what I mean?" said Kicsi. She folded the knapsack and put it back in the wall. The cat walked disdainfully away. "There's always something."

"Well," said Aladár. "You'd better go, I guess. I hope— can I see you again tomorrow?"

"Oh, yes," said Kicsi. She took a deep breath. No more secrets, she thought. "I like you," she said.

"I like you too," said Aladár. "Good-bye."

But the next day she woke to loud and piercing screams. She heard Imre's voice in the living room, and then, from the next room, the sounds of Tibor getting dressed.

"What is it?" said Ilona sleepily. She had always been a heavy sleeper. "What *time* is it?"

"I don't know," Kicsi said. "Come on, get dressed. There's something going on."

"All right. All right, in a minute. You go on."

She dressed quickly and followed Imre, Sarah, and Tibor outside. The town was dark and still, but the dawn was coming soon. Soft circles of lamplight fell against the graveled streets. Up ahead Kicsi saw the lamplighter, following the crowd to the synagogue.

"It's locked," said someone.

"What's going on?"

"Get the sexton, he has the keys."

Through the crowd Kicsi caught sight of Aladár, standing near the synagogue with Erzsébet's family. She ran to him.

"Does this happen a lot in your village?" Aladár said. "Golems and demons and rabbi's curses— It's crazy." He shook his head. "This doesn't happen where I come from." He broke off as the rabbi ran up the street, followed by the sexton. "He runs fast for such an old man, doesn't he?" Aladár whispered.

"Shhh," said Kicsi. "It's just someone locked in the building." She hoped fiercely that it was, that it wasn't what she had thought at first. That it wasn't Vörös, or Vörös's soul.

The screams from the synagogue were louder now. Like most of the townspeople, Kicsi had not had time to put on heavy clothes and shoes; she stood shivering in the cold as the sexton opened the old synagogue doors.

A man with thin arms and legs and a rounded belly came to the door. A few of the townspeople began to laugh, or to turn away.

"Who's that?" Aladár whispered.

"That's the village no-good," said Kicsi.

"What? Who?"

"Wait a minute," said Kicsi. "I think he's trying to tell us something."

The no-good opened his mouth, but no sound came out. Then: "Dead," he whispered.

"What?" said the sexton impatiently. He held the other man by the arm and pulled him out of the building, then locked the doors. "You shouldn't have been in there," he said. "What happened? Did you get locked in?"

"Dead," the man repeated. "I was in there with them all night, all the dead ones. All of them dead."

"Who are, uncle?" said someone in the crowd.

"All of them," said the no-good. "A—a man on a horse. A tall man. And someone with a candle, and someone with a sword. And there was a man, a man with a crown, and— and lights in his eyes. And a woman with water streaming through her hair, and her eyes—no, I won't say what her eyes were like. But she looked at me, I'll say that much." He backed against the doors and nearly collapsed against them. His next words were so low they could barely be heard. "That's when I started to scream."

László, an old man, spat on the ground three times. "An omen," Sholom said, his voice low with fear.

The no-good's teeth were chattering and he could not say another word. "Come on," the sexton said, not unkindly. "I'll take you home. You could do with some food. Let's go."

"What do you make of that?" said Imre.

"He's always been slightly crazy," said István, Erzsébet's father. He was a heavyset man with a red face. "I wouldn't worry about him."

"But not like this," said Imre. "Hungry, sometimes, and dirty, yes, but he's never seen ghosts. Someone with a candle . . . I wonder what it means."

The crowd began to break apart. László hurried past.

"It's an omen, that's what it means," he said. "A death in the village. Sholom was right."

István shrugged. "Uncle's got a good meal and a place to sleep nights," he said. "I don't think there's any more to it than that."

"You don't think it was any kind of warning?" said Imre.

"Warning? I don't think so. The rabbi would know. He—" István looked around. "Strange," he said. "He was here, wasn't he? I wonder where he went."

Ilona joined them, her face flushed with sleep. "What do you think?" she said to Kicsi. "Is he crazy or did he really see—"

"I don't know," said Kicsi. "Erzsébet's father thinks he's crazy."

"What about the rabbi?" said Aladár.

"The rabbi? I don't know. What does he say?"

"He doesn't," said Aladár. "He's disappeared."

"Disappeared?" said Ilona. "When?"

"He hasn't disappeared," said Kicsi. "He's just gone home."

"Probably back to sleep," said Ilona. "That's what I'd do. I'll see you later." She hurried away.

"He disappeared," said Aladár again. "I saw him looking inside the synagogue, and when I looked again he was gone."

"That doesn't mean anything," said Kicsi.

"What do you mean, it doesn't mean anything?" said Aladár. "You know what he can do. And what about the dead in the synagogue? What is he doing?"

"I don't know." Kicsi shook her head. "Why would he disappear? It doesn't make sense."

"He knows something," said Aladár. He stopped. They had reached Erzsébet's house. "We have to follow him. Watch him."

"We do? Why?"

"You did it before, didn't you?"

"I—Yes, I did, but that was different. That was because of Vörös. I don't want to follow the rabbi. He's—he's dangerous. It's not safe."

"I'll do it alone, then," said Aladár. "You don't have to come if you don't want to."

"No. All right. I'll do it if you want," said Kicsi slowly.

"I have to go home. I didn't even have breakfast yet. I'll see you later."

"All right," said Aladár. "Good-bye. And thanks!"

He was waiting for her when she left the house nearly an hour later. "Where do we start?" he asked, coming to meet her. "His house or the synagogue?"

"I've been thinking," said Kicsi. "What if he just went home without anyone noticing? Wouldn't we look silly?"

"He didn't," said Aladár. "You know he didn't. Kicsi." He looked at her seriously. "Are you afraid?"

"Afraid?" she said. "Well, yes. I am. You haven't seen him when he does magic. You think it's all a game."

"It's all right," said Aladár. "I'm afraid too. Where do you want to start?"

"The—the synagogue, I guess."

"You'd better show me the way, then."

They set off together. The day was hot for early spring. Yellow daffodils grew by the side of the road. They saw no one as they passed Sholom's house and the graveyard, and came at last to the synagogue. Kicsi thought of the time the glass had shattered in the courtyard, thought of Vörös's warning, and she shivered against the heat.

"It's locked," said Aladár, trying the door. "He's not here."

They stood awhile, looking at the heavy doors.

"Listen," said Kicsi. "Do you hear anything?"

"What?"

"A—murmuring sound. Like a crowd of people far away."

"It's the wind," Aladár said. "Isn't it?"

"I don't think so," said Kicsi. "Let's go."

"Where?"

"To his house. I don't think—I don't think that we're safe here. That we're safe alone."

"All right," said Aladár.

He followed her along the winding road back to the rabbi's house. Suddenly she stopped. "Look," she said.

Through a window at the side of the house they could see the rabbi. He was bent over his desk, looking through a book with a cracked leather binding. Piles of old books were stacked to either side of him. As they watched, he put on his glasses and bent closer to the book.

"You were right," said Aladár, whispering. "He's just studying."

"No," said Kicsi. "Can you see the books? Careful! What language are they in? Is it—Hebrew?"

"I can't—wait. Wait a minute." Aladár moved forward slowly, until he was almost at the windowsill. "I don't know," he said, coming back to her. "I think so."

"He's learning their names," said Kicsi.

"What?"

"Shhh. The dead. He has to learn their names to have power over them."

The rabbi looked up at his desk. The sun outside the window threw the shadow of his glasses onto his face, so that for a moment he looked like a demon with huge staring eyes. Kicsi and Aladár stood still, rapt with fear.

"Come on," Aladár said urgently, taking her arm. "Let's go. Pretend we were just passing by."

Kicsi began to move. She glanced at Aladár, who still held her arm. Had he said that he was frightened too? He didn't seem to be afraid.

They turned the corner, still walking slowly. "That was close," said Aladár. "What do you mean? Why does he have to learn their names?"

"Just a minute," said Kicsi. She was shaking. "Let me sit down. Do you think he saw us?"

"I don't think so." Aladár sat down beside her. "Let's rest here awhile. What did you mean about the names?"

"Names have power. If he learns their names he can control them," said Kicsi. "That's what Vörös told me. Vörös never told me his real name."

"What do you think he'll do next? The rabbi, I mean. Do you think he'll go to the synagogue?"

"I guess so. Let's stay here awhile. Until he leaves."

"All right. What else did Vörös tell you? Is that where the rabbi gets his power? From names?"

"From words. Sometimes even from letters. Every Hebrew letter is also a number. And all the letters in a word add up to another number. Some words are equal to each other. Some are worth more than others. It's all very complicated." Aladár looked at her in amazement. "Well, actually I didn't learn that from Vörös. I read it in a book once. The magic is called Kabbalah. I didn't understand most of it." She laughed. "I guess I can see now why the rabbi didn't want us to learn Hebrew in school. It could be dangerous."

"And what about Vörös?" said Aladár. "Is that where he gets his power too?"

"I don't know," Kicsi said. "I think so." She looked around the corner. "The door's opening. Come on, let's go."

Kicsi and Aladár waited until the rabbi started down the street and then followed him. He came to the synagogue and stopped, listening intently. They quickly hid across the street, behind a clump of trees.

The rabbi pressed his palms against the synagogue doors and said a few words. He took a key from a ring at his belt and opened the doors slowly.

At first Kicsi and Aladár could see only darkness inside the synagogue. Then, within the darkness, they made out winking forms of light. "Look," said Aladár. "The man with a crown." Golden points of a crown gleamed in the blackness.

"A woman," said Kicsi. "With a silver sword." The fine edge of the sword flashed up out of the darkness like a ribbon of light.

"Listen," said Aladár. The dead figures murmured to each other, crowding toward the light.

The rabbi held up his hand. "Stop," he said.

The dead fell silent, watchful, listening.

"I know your names," the rabbi said. "I know you all. You are the murdered, the unavenged dead, come from across time. You cannot sleep until you have had your revenge." One of the dead moaned, a deep chilling sound that Kicsi felt in her bones. "You will not move. You will not move until I have finished!" the rabbi said, and the sound stopped.

"Old tales say that you appeared before the great catastrophes. But the old tales contain exaggerations, and often lie. I will not believe that we are doomed. But you are here, and I will make my own use of you. I will bind you to the village for my own purposes."

The dead flowed to the door, chains and jewels and swords winking out of the darkness.

"You will not get out," said the rabbi. "I put a spell on the door, the strongest binding I know. Here in the synagogue I am master. You cannot get out."

The dead stopped. The rabbi began to speak, chanting

quickly the names of the dead. "And so I bind you," he said. "Here you will stay until I release you. Sleep now, until I call."

The dead melted back into the darkness. The rabbi closed the door and locked it. "That should take care of the traveling man," he said. "That Vörös." He walked away quickly, making no sound as he went.

"Well," said Aladár. His voice shook a little. "I don't think I'll doubt your stories again."

"Yes," said Kicsi. "But what about—what about Vörös? He'll never be able to come back to the village now."

"You'll find some way to get to him, to warn him in time."

"I hope so," said Kicsi. "I hope I can."

"We could go down to the forest," said Aladár, "and leave him something. A note, maybe. Or something from his knapsack."

"Do you think so?" said Kicsi. Her eyes shone. "We could do that tomorrow. Or—no, I have to help my mother around the house tomorrow. I promised her I would. What about the day after?"

"I'm leaving then," said Aladár. "In the morning."

"So soon?" said Kicsi. "Are you—are you coming back?"

"Of course," said Aladár. "Why—did you think I wouldn't?"

"Everyone's always leaving," said Kicsi. "Vörös, and now you . . ."

"I'm not a traveling magician," said Aladár. "I'll be back."

"All right," said Kicsi. "Next year?"

"Next year," said Aladár solemnly, a promise.

"I'll meet you at Erzsi's house before you leave," said Kicsi. "We can say good-bye then."

"No," said Aladár. "Let's say good-bye now. It'll be harder in front of so many people."

"Now?" said Kicsi. "I guess so. All right."

"Good-bye, then," said Aladár. He looked around carefully to make sure no one was watching and then kissed her quickly.

"Good-bye . . ." she said, wonderingly. He hurried away toward Erzsébet's house before she could say anything else. He did not look back.

Then all that was left to her was to count the days until

the next Passover. She grew taller and leaner, and began to walk slower than she used to, as though she were going somewhere important but was in no hurry to get there. She did her schoolwork and housework quickly and well, and no one suspected that she was miles away from the small village.

One evening shortly after Aladár left she came downstairs to say good night to her parents. They were listening to the radio and had not heard her. Imre turned to Sarah and said, "I don't know."

"Is it bad? Should we try to leave? Remember what Vörös said—" said Sarah.

"Vörös? He's been gone nearly a year. And I still don't know about that man—a part of me says not to trust him, but all the while I know I would give him whatever he asked for—my house and my honor . . ." His voice trailed off. He looked at a spot on the far wall. "But no, I don't think we should leave. Where would we go? At least here we have the printing company, and our neighbors. . . . Surely they can't do anything against so many of us."

Kicsi moved suddenly. "Kicsi!" said Sarah. The parents looked at each other and then looked quickly away. "I didn't see you there. Did you come to say good night?"

"Yes," said Kicsi, wondering what it was that they didn't want to talk about in front of her. "Good night." Then she said suddenly, "Have you ever had a dream about a man with no teeth?"

"A man with no teeth?" said Sarah, laughing. "No, Kicsi, why do you ask?"

"I do sometimes. Last night. And Vörös did."

This time Imre and Sarah could not look at each other. The silence in the room lengthened like shadows. "Well, good night," Kicsi said again, and she turned and ran upstairs.

"Vörös again," said Imre. "I wonder just what it is that man knew. And if he knew that we were in danger, why on earth did he leave us?"

Summer passed, and autumn. Kicsi returned often to the forest, watching the trees grow and fade with the seasons, watching the new seedlings bind over the scars from the fire. One day when she came home from the forest she saw a letter on the dining room table. It was addressed to her, from Aladár. She tore it open.

It was very short. Aladár was well and getting along in his studies. At the bottom he had written, "I look forward to seeing you again." She reread the letter, then took it to her room. She read it every day after that, until the places where it was folded began to tear.

The snows that year came early, and with them bitter cold. Coming home from school one day Kicsi saw her father and István, standing and talking with a man who had his back to her. She ran to greet her father, her breath puffing in the cold, but stopped when she recognized the other man. It was the rabbi.

"Hello, Kicsi," said Imre. "Come here and we'll walk home together."

Kicsi came reluctantly. The rabbi nodded at her, but said nothing. His gray eyes were light, almost transparent. "I have wonderful news," he said to Imre and István. "My daughter is going to have a child."

"Mazel tov!" said Imre.

"Yes, I'm very grateful," said the rabbi. "I feared for her life, you know, after the—after the wedding. And then I began to fear that she would never have a child. But that traveler, that Vörös, apparently he was not as clever as he appeared to be. Because my child is well, despite his words."

"Well, then," said István. "Do you think Vörös will return?"

"I don't have any idea. I don't dictate his comings and goings. You, Imre—you were friendly with him at one time—if you see him, tell him he may return, if he chooses."

"Vörös!" said Imre. "No one in the village seems to be able to talk about anything else, even though he's been gone for over a year. Sometimes I think you're right—he's not as clever as he seems. Why should he come back now? We're getting along here without him." Imre sighed. "But other times—I just wish I knew."

"I don't think he'll be coming back," said the rabbi. "The village is as peaceful as it's ever been. For a long time now I've felt that I would like to go on a long trip—see what my colleagues are doing in the outside world. I think I will start soon, after the snow melts. And as for my daughter, doctor"—he nodded toward István—"I will leave her in your competent hands." He nodded to Imre and walked away, his feet making no sound in the snow.

And then, almost before Kicsi expected it, Passover came around once again. Since of the sisters only she and Ilona were left at home, she was allowed her first new dress. Almost breathless, she took off her school clothes and put them away. As she turned toward the bed where she had laid the new dress, she saw something gleam in the corner of her eye. She walked over to the mirror. It was her star, glowing a pale silver.

Vörös! She had almost forgotten him. Though everyone in the village seemed to be worried about something, the danger he had spoken of had not come to pass. She felt almost a little guilty, to think that she had forgotten the man she had once loved, the man who carried magic with him as he moved through the world, and she felt sad, too, to think that she had nearly grown up—stories of faraway places could no longer move her as they once had.

Then she put on the dress, slowly, carefully. She would see Aladár again tonight!

Kicsi went downstairs. Sarah was setting out the Passover dishes. She had invited Erzsébet's family to dinner, in part to get to know Aladár better, since Kicsi had spent so much time with him last year. Magda was celebrating with her husband's family.

Someone knocked on the front door. "Kicsi!" called Sarah "Get the door, will you please? I'm busy here."

Kicsi opened the door. Erzsébet, her brother, and her parents came in; last of all came Aladár. Kicsi looked at him and could not speak. He looked so fine in his new suit. He was taller than she remembered. They could not embrace with everyone around them. He smiled at her and shrugged, as if to say it couldn't be helped.

The candles flickered in the wind. Kicsi closed the door.

"Good God, but it's dark out there!" István said to Imre, who had just come into the room. His family seated themselves on the couch.

"The lamplighter's gone," said Imre, sitting in one of the overstuffed chairs.

"Gone?" said István. "Where to?"

Imre shrugged. "I don't know," he said. "And he's not the only one. The shoemaker left yesterday."

"Where do they all go?"

"Who knows? They think they'll be safe somewhere else."

"The rabbi's gone," said István.

"The rabbi?" said Imre. "He's on vacation. He'll be coming back."

"Of course. Of course he will. Still, the rabbi's a strange man. He knows what he wants, and he's used to getting it. Remember the time he cursed the school—" István stopped. He had never before mentioned the curse to Imre; István had been one of the men who had ostracized Imre and his family when Imre had continued to send his children to the school.

Imre shrugged. His paralyzed hand lay heavily in his lap. He did not hold a grudge against anyone. "But he wouldn't leave his wife and daughter, if he thinks that there's any danger. And with his daughter pregnant—"

"No," said István. "No, of course you're right."

Sarah came into the room. "Shall we go sit down?" she asked.

Chapter

6

Kicsi sat across from Aladár; between them was a silver candelabrum. Next to her Erzsébet talked of school and other friends. Imre, at the head of the table, began the tale of Passover—"We were slaves in the land of Egypt," he said—as he did every year. But it seemed to her that she could only see Aladár, dimly, through the points of light that separated them like a flickering bead curtain.

As Imre ended, she got up and helped Sarah carry the food from the kitchen. She carried a platter full of chicken past Aladár. "How have you been?" she asked. "How's college?"

"I've been fine," he said. "College is wonderful. I think —I've been thinking about becoming an engineer."

"An engineer?" said István, helping himself to salad. "I thought you wanted to be a doctor."

"I did, but—"

"Kicsi!" Sarah called from the kitchen. Kicsi sighed. Maybe she would get to talk to Aladár some other time.

Sarah had worked all day on the meal. There were many courses, and all of them were praised. As the meal ended, Imre continued with the Passover services. He nodded to István to open the door, as the custom was, to let in those who were hungry, or those who had no place to go on this night.

The candles had burned low. Aladár caught Kicsi's eye and whispered, "Have you seen Vörös? Did he come back?"

"No," she whispered. "I didn't really think he would."

István went to the front door and opened it. The night was very cold, and the sky was black and hard, starless. The streets were empty. István shivered. No one in the dining room could see him. Apologetically, he began to close the door.

Someone knocked. "Who is it?" Imre called from the dining room.

"I don't know," said István. His face was bloodless and his hands shook. Cautiously, he opened the door.

A man in a uniform stood there. "Hello," he said in accented Hungarian. "Are you the master of the house?"

"Nooo . . ." said István. He shook his head suddenly and said briskly, "Come this way." He led the man into the dining room.

Imre stood up. "Yes?" he said. "What do you want?"

The man looked down at a piece of paper in his hand. "You are ordered to report to the brick factory near the railroad tracks next Wednesday," he said. "Twenty-six April, nineteen forty-four."

"Me?" said Imre. "I—I am ordered—"

"No," said the man in uniform. He looked around the table. "All of you. All the Jews in the village." He smiled suddenly. He had no teeth.

Kicsi cried out. The man in uniform ignored her.

"You— By what right— You cannot—" said Imre. He sat down slowly.

"Why, yes, we can," the man said. He looked at Imre as if he thought Imre were slow-witted. "Of course we can. Look here. We have our orders." He showed Imre the piece of paper he carried.

The paper was in German; it meant nothing to Imre. He waved it away. "What about—well, the printing press. The house, and—and—things," he finished. He shrugged, one shoulder higher than the other because of his paralyzed arm. He was almost apologetic.

"I really don't know," said the man. "I suppose we will take possession of it as soon as you leave."

"And if we refuse to go?" said Aladár.

"Ali!" said Erzsébet.

"You won't be allowed to escape, I can tell you that," said the man. "It will be easier for you if you just do as we say.

"Next Wednesday," he added unnecessarily, as he turned to go. It was only then that they all saw the gun he carried under his belt.

"What—what in God's name will we do?" Sarah whispered when the soldier had left.

"What can we do?" said Imre. "We'll have to go. Of course we'll have to go." He spoke tonelessly. "What can they do to us?"

Kicsi had never seen her stubborn father at such a loss, had never seen him apologize when not in the wrong. She turned to him, to plead with him to be strong. Blackness seemed to be filling her world, shutting out the lights between her and Aladár, filling the spaces behind her eyes.

Erzsébet's family went home early. There was no singing after the meal as there would have been in other years, no conversation as they went out into the streets that wound away like black rivers under the sky. "What can they do to us?" said everyone, and they shrugged and turned to go.

By Wednesday they were still saying it; it had become a password. No one knew how much they were allowed to take with them, so Sarah packed clothes for all of them. Before she left she watered the plants and fed the cat; then she started to cry.

"Come with me, my heart," Imre said to her, and put his arm softly around her shoulders.

Kicsi and Aladár walked hand in hand, not speaking, to the factory. A guard at the factory separated them. The men were to go to one building and the women to another.

"Good-bye," said Aladár. "I know I'll see you again. Don't worry."

"I won't," said Kicsi, though she had none of his confidence. "Good-bye."

They kissed and separated. Kicsi saw the guard as she turned to join Sarah and Ilona. There was something in his face that might have been kindness, or pity. As she looked at him he turned away, embarrassed. So, Kicsi thought, they are not all like the man we saw last week, the man with no teeth. She shivered, and hurried toward her mother.

The warehouse was large and dark and drafty. It seemed full of hundreds and hundreds of women. They stood nervously in groups, or sat against piles of bricks, or lay wearily on the floor. Their voices echoed off the walls. Some carried small children. Kicsi finally saw Sarah, standing with a group of people talking to the rabbi's daughter. She slipped next to her and hung on to her dress like a young child. "Kicsi," said Sarah, smiling at her.

"When will you have the child?" said someone.

"Another month or so," said the rabbi's daughter. "I don't know—there aren't any doctors here, are there? If István were here—but he isn't, is he?" She looked around the warehouse vaguely, but did not seem disappointed not to find him. "Something will turn up, I guess. I hope they'll give me enough to feed the baby."

But night came on and no one showed up with food. Some of the women complained, calling out that they were hungry. Guards came in with guns and singled out the ones who had been the loudest. These were shoved roughly out the door and on to cattle cars waiting on the railroad tracks. Everyone else quieted that night and went to sleep —on the cold, damp brick floors—hungry.

The next day they were each given a slice of bread. More cars came and more of the women were led away. Those who stayed quiet in the hopes of being ignored were disappointed; women were chosen at random. One, a small girl with long brown hair, was dragged screaming to the tracks. A guard clenched her hair and carried her along as if she were a dog.

Days went by. More cars came up to the warehouse, and more women were taken away. They were hungry all the time, but nearly everyone shared their food with the rabbi's daughter. She had sunk within herself, down to a universe that contained only her and the unborn baby. Her cheeks were hollow and her skin was white as paper.

One day Ilona said to Kicsi, "Have you heard about Aladár?"

"Ali!" said Kicsi. "No, what happened?"

"He tried to escape. Last night."

"Tried? Did he—what did they do to him?" They were whispering. They all whispered to hoard their strength.

"They caught him. And—and they sent him away, this morning."

"And—and what? Is that all they did?" Ilona was concealing something.

"No," she said slowly. "They beat him first. His face was bloody. He could barely move."

"How do you know?" said Kicsi. "Did you see him?"

"Someone had seen him. She told me."

"Oh! Oh, Ali . . ." Kicsi sat down. She could not think. There was a buzzing in her ears all the time now. She was very hungry. "He said he'd see me again . . ."

"He will," said Ilona. She repeated the old question. "What can they do to us?" The question seemed to mock her.

The next morning the guard pointed to Kicsi. "You," he said. "And you, and you, and you." Sarah and the rabbi's daughter and Ilona. They were taken outside.

Bright spots multiplied in front of Kicsi's eyes. The sun seemed to slide in every direction. It was a relief to get outside, after so many days in the warehouse, but she was quickly taken into one of the cattle cars.

The car smelled of straw and cows and human sweat. More and more people were crowded into the car; soon everyone was crying out that there was no room, and still more people joined them. Kicsi found herself in a corner, next to the rabbi's daughter. At first they had tried to clear some room for the pregnant woman, but the space they had made was quickly filled.

The train began to move. Someone bumped into Kicsi, cried out, and was stilled. The car grew hotter. There was no food, and no one had eaten since the day before. The passengers huddled together, moaning softly. Kicsi dozed off, woke, dozed, and woke. Asleep or awake, the rhythm of the train on the tracks stitched itself into her mind.

The train stopped. The doors were opened, and the passengers looked up, blinking in the light. Someone stood up.

"Don't," said the guard at the door. He held up his rifle, ill at ease. The woman sat back down. The guard passed in a pail of water, locked the doors, and left. The train started up again.

The water was passed around. Everyone drank thirstily, and the pail was passed around again, but there was nothing left when it reached Kicsi the second time.

The days blended into one another. Sometimes once a day, sometimes every few hours, the doors would open and more water would be passed in. Through a crack in the door the passengers could see that they were moving past endless fields. Towns rose up before them like islands and were passed by.

Once the train stopped and the doors did not open. The passengers waited an endless time, sitting still, watching the door. Those who were sleeping stirred and woke. The car grew unbearably hot. A woman near Kicsi fainted, and someone Kicsi could not see was sick. The smell of vomit filled the car.

"Where are they taking us?" called someone desperately, and another voice answered, "They are taking us to die." The rabbi's daughter, shocked out of her apathy, began to scream, and soon she was joined by hundreds and hundreds of voices, some screaming, some crying frantically. The sounds echoed off the iron walls of the car.

"Quiet!" someone said, banging her hand against the side of the car. "We are not going to die. Don't be ridiculous. Why should they kill us? Lie down and save your strength. Go to sleep."

A few people quieted, and more followed. Soon only a handful were left, moaning softly and rocking back and forth in their small spaces. Then the train began to move again.

A few days later the train stopped and the doors were flung open. They had arrived at evening, and they strained to see against the setting sun. A cloud of smoke filled the sky, burning against the sunset like a wall of red flame. They heard dogs barking, and men firing rifles, and far off, the sound of people screaming.

Then the dogs were upon them, forcing families apart, herding everyone in one direction. Guards shouted in German. The prisoners could see where they were going now—toward a squat row of buildings punctuated by watchtowers and by tall chimneys spouting flame. Enormous strands of barbed wire wound along the tops of fences and around the buildings.

The prisoners were forced through the entrance, a huge empty hallway crowded with people. Kicsi saw with horror what seemed to her to be a living skeleton, a man made of bone and shadows. What have they done to him? she thought. Someone nudged her and said, "We'll all look like that soon."

"Strip," said a woman in uniform, and, dazed, they all bent to remove their clothing. "Shoes go in that pile over there, clothes over here. Any possessions you brought with you go over there. Jewelry in this pile. Come on, hurry up! What are you waiting for?"

A pile of dull gold and silver, of winking rubies and sapphires and emeralds, lay jumbled together on the floor. A rope of pearls wound around them, grinning up at Kicsi like a skull's teeth.

Kicsi's hand went to her throat, to the clasp of the necklace she always wore. Rapidly she undid the clasp, slid the star into the palm of her left hand, and held her hand loosely at her side, as if she were concealing nothing. Vörös! she thought, and was surprised to realize that she had not thought of him before. You were right. Oh, why didn't we listen to you? There was danger to the village, terrible danger. You made the golem to save us, to destroy the man with no teeth. You told me that maybe I could be saved. Maybe, if I have the necklace.

The prisoners were given shirts and pants made of flimsy cloth, and worn shoes. Kicsi put them on awkwardly, trying to hide her left hand. The woman in uniform waved them on into the next room.

"Next," she said. Kicsi stepped up. "All right, you can go. Straight through that door there."

Kicsi began to walk away. "Wait a minute," the woman said. "Your hand. No, the other hand. Let me see it. Do I have to open it myself?"

Slowly Kicsi opened her hand and showed the woman the star. The silver glistened in the dim light. "Ah, I thought so. Here. Give it here. Oh, don't be childish." The woman put her hand on the star and turned to go. The star did not move.

"What? What is this? Don't play games with me, young lady, or I will see to it that you are not so fortunate in the next room. Give me your necklace."

Around them people were moving, begging to keep just one trinket, crying softly. Another train pulled up outside and the dogs began to bark again. Kicsi heard none of it. The world had narrowed down to her and the woman in uniform and the star in the palm of her hand. Blood sang in her ears.

The woman tried once more to take the necklace. "Have

you got it glued to your hand, then?" she said. Her eyes narrowed. She pulled harder. A drop of red blood appeared at one of the points of the star and clouded the silver. Kicsi cried out in pain. The star began to come loose, leaving deep welts where it had been. Blood welled up from the scars.

The woman in uniform hissed. "Witchcraft!" she said, looking at the bloody necklace in her hand. She tosssed it quickly into the pile of jewelry. "You're a witch!"

Kicsi stared numbly at her palm. Beneath the running blood she could see the faint outline of the star, and she knew she would have the scar for life. Perhaps it was true then. Perhaps she was a witch. She often knew things without knowing how she knew. And Sholom—hadn't he once said that she had been touched by magic? Oh, Vörös, she thought. What is happening to all of us?

"Go on into the next room, witch," said the woman in uniform. "They know what to do with people like you there."

In the next room were several men. Only one of them spoke. When she got close enough to hear what he was saying she saw that he said only two words. "Left," he said. "Right. Right. Left." As each prisoner came up to him he indicated the direction they were to go. "Left," he said monotonously. "Left. Right."

Up ahead Kicsi could see Sarah. She had not seen her mother since leaving the cattle car. "Left," the man said, but not to Sarah. It was as if he thought Sarah could not understand him. A guard moved her over to the left.

"Right," he said in the same tone as Ilona stepped up to him. "Left," to the rabbi's daughter. He studied Kicsi. Her left hand was clenched against the pain. Finally, "Right," he said.

Those on the right were taken to the barracks—low buildings that contained beds built like shelves for hundreds and hundreds of people. "This is where you will stay," said a guard.

Night had fallen, and the prisoners could see people stacked like wood, sleeping fitfully. A few had woken when they heard the guard.

"What—what happened to the others?" said someone.

"Them?" he said. "They came in through the doors, but

they'll go out through the furnaces." He studied the small group of women. "Just as you will. Just as you will."

"But why?"

"Why? They were too old, or too sick, or too young. Troublemakers."

"No, I meant why—" someone said. Kicsi did not hear her. A roaring built up like a wave inside her. Troublemakers. That meant Aladár. He was dead. She had known it from the time they had said good-bye. Aladár was dead, and she was a witch, someone who had been touched by magic. How else had she known with such certainty that he would die? And Sarah, and poor Imre with his paralyzed arm—they were dead. All of them dead.

The world folded over like paper, and the other side was blank, was empty. She sank gratefully into that emptiness, and for a long time she knew no more.

They had shaved her head to prevent lice, but she had lice anyway. Her teeth had begun to hurt, and she was hungry all the time. She could not wash herself, and her clothes and skin were caked over with mud and ashes from the furnaces. The scar on her palm had never healed, but had remained the color of old blood.

Every few weeks the barracks would be visited by guards, and a few people taken away. She did not know where the people went, and she did not try to find out. She said nothing to anyone, and the others ignored her.

One day a few months later she was among those taken away. She was led outside and put on another train heading to another camp. During the trip a prisoner died of the heat, and no one came to collect his body. As soon as the doors were opened the prisoners flung the corpse outside.

Because Kicsi was quiet and docile she was given what was considered a good job: she was to work in the kitchen squad. "Get us some food—a carrot, maybe, or some bread," they would say to her, the people that slept in the barracks with her, and they would try to bribe her with cigarettes, with the promise of the use of a toothbrush. She did not hear them. She went to work, often for twenty hours a day, came back to the crowded room and slept, and went to work with the dawn, woken by the dogs. Occasionally she would eat from the food she was preparing, but she did not remember it.

The kitchen workers were watched by guards, and no one spoke. Everyone was tired and hungry. A few were sick, but they tried to work anyway. The smoke from the furnaces was everywhere; it rose to the sky and blotted out the stars, and it reminded them of what would happen to them if they could not work.

One day Kicsi heard laughter in the kitchen, and she looked up, surprised. A short bandy-legged man with dark black hair and eyes had come in and given the guard a piece of paper. The guard shifted his rifle and read the paper slowly, and over his shoulder the short man mimicked him with exaggerated gestures. The guard looked up, and the laughter stopped suddenly.

"It says here you were a *Feuermann,* a stoker," said the guard.

"Yes, that's right," said the short man.

"And that you're to be transferred to the kitchens," the guard went on, slowly. He sounded puzzled.

"That's right."

"Why?"

"Why?" said the short man, amused. He shrugged, as if to say, Who knows why they do anything around here? "I don't know."

"All right, then, get to work. Get that bucket over there and boil some potatoes. And don't expect me to tell you what to do after that, because I won't. You find your own work."

The short man nodded and turned to work, and quiet settled among the workers again.

A few minutes later the woman next to Kicsi was laughing softly. Kicsi stopped her work and moved closer to her. The short man was spinning her a tale about an elaborate black-market scheme he had set up, about the ways he planned to sell the food he was going to steal from the kitchens. As he finished the woman wiped her eyes with her sleeve and sighed.

"Ah, that's good, my friend," she said. "You almost make me believe we will get out of here alive."

Kicsi went back to cutting potatoes.

The short man whistled as he worked. At first the guard frowned at him, but he did not threaten him, and the man continued to whistle. Kicsi found that she could ignore the short man, could turn the whistling into background noise.

For weeks he whistled the same tune over and over; then suddenly he began to sing the words.

> "Naming names the wisest know,
> Soft he'll come and softly go,
> Taking one or two away,
> Comforting the ones who stay.
>   When you're doing all you can,
>   You'll see him come—the red-haired man."

Kicsi looked up. Her throat was full of unspoken words, and she was painfully close to crying. She tried to speak, but could not. The short man began to sing again.

> "Passing forest, passing field,
> Unheralded and unrevealed,
> He comes to comfort we who stay,
> And takes one or two away—"

"What—what do you mean?" said Kicsi. Her voice was dry. No one heard her. She cleared her throat. "What do you mean, about the red-haired man?"

The short man turned to her and shrugged. "Nothing. I don't know. It's just a song."

"Where did you hear it? What does it mean?"

"Over at the barracks. They say—" He looked around him and lowered his voice. "Well, a friend of mine said— I know this sounds crazy—he said that there's this man. A red-haired man, a traveler. A sort of magician. You can see him sometimes, standing out past the barbed wire, and then all of a sudden—*poof!*—he's inside. And he takes you out with him. He—my friend—he taught me the song."

The short man was silent for a while. "Then—yesterday —my friend disappeared. I know—I know they took him away, to—you know—to be killed. But I can't help myself. I think that he met the red-haired man, and that he's safe now."

"I know him," said Kicsi. "The red-haired man. Your friend is safe."

"*You* know him? How?"

"He was—he was a friend of my family. A friend of mine. I haven't seen him now for—oh, for years. But I know your friend is safe. He was a magician—a very good magician."

"A magician? But—how do you know?"

Kicsi held out her palm. She had never shown her scar to anyone, had tried to keep it hidden. "He gave me this," she said.

"He *gave* you—" The short man looked at her in amazement. His eyes lost their laughter, became confused.

A guard looked up. Kicsi turned back to the stove. Her face had gone wooden, dead. When the guard looked away, the short man turned to Kicsi and said, "What on earth did you mean by that?"

Kicsi said nothing. It was as if she had never spoken.

The next day the short man was gone. Kicsi did not know if he had been taken to the ovens or if he had met the red-haired man. She did not ask. She did her work and went back to the barracks to sleep.

That night she dreamt about Vörös. She saw Ilona and Sarah and the rabbi's daughter being herded onto cattle cars, exactly as before, but this time Vörös stood at the doors. She reached for her necklace, knowing that if she showed it to him she would not have to get into the train. The necklace was gone. She fumbled for it wildly, knowing that it had to be there. The red-haired man looked at her and said, "In that case, you will have to go with the others." He smiled. He had no teeth.

Kicsi screamed. She woke up and lay for a moment without opening her eyes, trying to pretend that she was still back in the village with her family and Vörös and that everything was as it had been before. Someone else in the barracks screamed, and another woman joined her; soon everyone was awake.

"It's all right," a woman on Kicsi's right said. She felt someone hold her hand. "You had a nightmare. You'll be all right now."

"Will you for God's sake stop that noise?" someone said loudly. Kicsi opened her eyes. A woman was climbing down from one of the upper beds. Her hair might have been brown once, though it was cut so short it was hard to tell, but it had begun to turn to gray. She did not look older than thirty-five.

The woman knelt down so that her eyes were level with Kicsi's. "What on earth is going on here, Rachel?"

"She had a nightmare," said Rachel. Then to Kicsi she said again, "It's all right now."

"My—my mother," said Kicsi. "And my sisters, and the man I was going to marry. They're dead now. All of them."

"The hell with them," said the gray-haired woman, not unkindly. "They're better off dead. We all would be." Rachel started to speak; she turned to her in anger. "And stop saying it's all right—it isn't all right and you know it. This young woman here has better sense than you." Someone wailed, a long keening note that stopped abruptly. "Now look what you've done. Once they get started they just don't stop."

"I—I'm sorry," said Kicsi. "I never realized before about —about—I never had a dream here until tonight, I think."

"You just realized that they're dead," said the gray-haired woman.

Kicsi nodded.

"And now you're trying to join them."

"What?"

"Well, look at you. Look at your hair—it's hard to keep it that dirty when it's cut so short, but you seem to manage. And look at your shoes. Winter is almost over and you haven't even tried to bind the holes. You'll freeze to death, if you don't die of stupidity first. You could at least wash yourself. You could pay some attention to what goes on around here. Someday you'll wake up to find you've sleepwalked right into the ovens. God, people make me sick sometimes. We should all die. It would be for the best."

"But what—how do I wash? They don't give us any—"

"Fool!" said the gray-haired woman, but Rachel said softly, "Some of us use the coffee they give us to wash in." She smiled. "You can't use it for drinking."

"Look around you, for God's sake," said the gray-haired woman. "We're all experts in survival. Even Rachel here."

"Why do you care?" said Kicsi suddenly, fiercely. Someone in the barracks began to cry. "If you hate people so much why don't you just kill yourself? Make it easier for them?"

"Why?" The gray-haired woman grinned triumphantly. "To spite them, that's why. Every day I stay alive is a victory. I don't worry about tomorrow."

"I try to stay alive because—well, so I can tell some-one," said Rachel. "To be a witness."

"Fool!" the other woman said again. "Who will you tell? You'll never get out of here. And even if you do, no one would believe you. Hell, I wouldn't believe it myself if any-one told me."

"Haven't you heard?" said Rachel. "The Germans are losing the war. We're going to be liberated."

The other woman laughed. "Liberated! We'll liberate ourselves, that's what. No one else will help us."

"Don't you hear the guns getting closer at night? And the planes, flying overhead? Why do you think they've got the furnaces going day and night now? They want to get rid of us before the British get here, so there won't be any-one left to tell our story."

"The furnaces?" The other woman yawned, stretched. "They want to kill us faster, that's all. I've got to get back to sleep—they give us little enough time as it is."

"Please," said Kicsi. "Could you tell me—"

"No," said the gray-haired woman. "I don't help anyone. It's the only way to stay alive." She climbed back up to her bed.

"Don't be angry with her," said Rachel. "They shot her children in front of her eyes. Two boys—they couldn't have been more than three years old." Then, in a whisper: "She doesn't know that I know. Don't tell her."

Kicsi nodded. "I wanted to ask her—how—how long have I been here?"

"I don't know," said Rachel. "You were here when I got here, and I've been here about six months. We both thought you wouldn't last long."

"Six months . . ." said Kicsi wonderingly. "I hardly re-member anything."

Suddenly she felt very tired. She rolled over and went to sleep.

The two women were gone when Kicsi woke the next day, but she remembered what they had told her. She watched as the prisoners were given what they called coffee, and when the guards looked away she rubbed some on her arms and legs. Stripes of dirt came away. Someone watch-ing her in the barracks silently gave her some rags to bind her shoes. She borrowed a comb from another woman, and the woman told her that she could use it once a week. Her hair covered her ears now, and it was almost to her eyes. When had it grown out? She remembered when they had shaved it, but little else. That was one of her last memories. And she remembered something else, too—the silky way her hair had felt before it was cut. She spent almost half an hour getting the snarls out, and she was nearly late for work. Suddenly it had become very important to stay alive.

The days passed into one another. Kicsi's hair grew out long and straight. She remembered Magda's curly black hair and how she had always envied her, but now she thought that there could be no hair in the world as fine as hers. She was the envy of the other prisoners; she had almost the longest hair in the barracks.

Once, when it was her turn to use the comb, the gray-haired woman said to her, "Look at that. You'd think your hair was the most important thing in the world."

"It is," said Kicsi, realizing it at that minute. She ran the comb carefully through her hair (she had broken one of the teeth last week) and smiled at the gray-haired woman. The woman gave her a smile back, though she frowned so quickly afterward that Kicsi was not sure that she had seen it.

Spring came, and people blessed the warmth, but there were no trees to mark the change in seasons. It was a year since Passover, but no one celebrated.

A day came when the prisoners were given no food or water. Another day passed like the first, and on the third day they were given only water. Kicsi survived by eating in the kitchen when the guards looked away. "You have to get us some food," said the gray-haired woman when Kicsi returned to the barracks that night.

"I know," said Kicsi. She looked to where Rachel slept on her cot, her face drawn and pale. "I'll try."

The next day, as she left the kitchen, she took with her a potato. That will do for me, she thought, and maybe for Rachel, but what about the gray-haired woman, and the woman who gives me her comb? She reached for a carrot, but her fingers trembled with hunger, and she dropped it.

"You there," said someone. "What have you got in your hand?" Hastily she tried to put the potato back. "Do you know what the penalty for stealing food is?" She nodded. She knew. They were going to shave her head.

"Come outside," the guard said, motioning with his rifle. She felt sick. Why had she taken the potato? She knew what the punishment was.

It was over quickly. The guard turned her over to the man who shaved the new arrivals. She watched numbly as the locks fell to the floor. With each new cut she felt she lost a part of herself. When it was over she could not bring herself to touch her head. She wanted only to fall back into the darkness, the safe, close darkness.

When they were through with her she returned to the barracks. Night had fallen; searchlights and smoke tarnished the sky. It was dimmer indoors, but she saw, through the afterimages of light, that the prisoners were having a sort of celebration. Food had come that evening, while Kicsi had been away.

"Kicsi," said the gray-haired woman. "What happened? We saved you some bread. What did they do—"

"We were so worried."

"My hair," Kicsi said, putting her hand up to her face. "They shaved it. I tried to steal some food."

"Kicsi," said Rachel. Kicsi noticed that she was looking better since the food had come. "You poor child. Thank you." She got up carefully and held Kicsi, touching her gently, caressing her where they had shaved her hair. Kicsi relaxed a little. The darkness had been put off for another day.

One night soon after, she woke with a fever. She threw her cover off but could not get comfortable. By morning she was shivering. She could not seem to see clearly, and people's voices sounded too high and too fast. Her body felt stiff and awkward as she dressed for work. At work she had to stop several times before she could force herself to go on.

That night, coming back from the kitchens, she thought she saw a man standing out beyond the barbed wire. He wavered like a mirage, fracturing with the landscape, coming closer and closer to the wire. The barbed wire shook like a plucked harp string, and he was inside.

Kicsi blinked, and he was gone.

The next day she could not get up. Two people argued above her like the Angel of Life and the Angel of Death. "Typhus," said one of them. She opened her eyes and saw the gray-haired woman.

94

"She has to go to work," said Rachel, on her other side. "They can't find her here. You know what they'll do to her if she can't work."

"I know," said the other woman. "Come on, now. Get up. You have to get up."

"I can't. . . ."

"Yes you can. Do you want to die?"

"Just go to work," said Rachel. "Other people will cover for you."

"No one will cover for her—they're all too busy staying alive themselves. Get into work, will you? I can't stay here and watch you forever."

Kicsi got up slowly. It was important to stay alive, to go to work and to stay clean and alert, but she could not remember why. Something that sounded like gunfire shook in her ears. The two women helped her dress. She walked slowly, concentrating on the movement of her legs. Somehow she made it to the kitchens.

"No work today," said the guard. "We're transporting people. Come on, everyone stay in line—"

"We'll be liberated soon," said a woman next to Kicsi. "That's why they're so nervous." She heard the guns again, in the distance.

"No talking!" said the guard. "Get in line. All right—I want you and you, and you over there. Everyone else stay here. Come on!"

The prisoners who were not chosen stood around awkwardly. "There aren't any guards here," someone said. "I wonder where they are. We could just—"

Kicsi did not hear. She had to lie down or she would die. No one was watching her. She went into the kitchen and stretched out on the floor. The world swam in front of her.

"The British!" someone shouted. "The British army is here!"

And someone else shouted, "We're alive!"

She did not hear. She was buried deep within her dreams.

Chapter

7

The tall red-haired man came into the camp in the late afternoon, stepping carefully over the bodies lying by the side of the road. A woman came up to meet him. As she drew nearer, he saw that she was a nurse.

"Is there something I can do for you?" she said.

"I was just about to ask you the same thing," he said. His English was strangely accented, but not unpleasant. "Can I do anything to help?"

"Can you?" said the nurse. "You're the answer to my prayers. Come with me."

She led him past a temporary shelter toward what had been the barracks. "Now what we've done here— Do you know anything about medicine?"

"A little."

"Good. What we've done is to divide the sick into three groups. The first group is well enough to be up and about —if they want anything they'll ask you for it. We've had a bit of a language problem, but we've found that a lot of them speak German or have learned enough to get by in the camps. Can you speak German?"

"Yes."

"Good," said the nurse, looking at him this time with

frank curiosity. "Then in what used to be the barracks we have the second group. These are the ones that will need medical attention—changing bandages, feeding, and so forth. Our worst problems seem to be typhus and malnutrition. And in the third group are those you saw by the road. We feel they're beyond help, and anyway we don't have enough medicine to see to everyone. It's a bad deal all round, but at least this way we're able to save some lives."

She led him back past the road toward the shelter. "Here's where we keep our supplies. Any medicine you check out has to be authorized by me or another of the head nurses. Right now that's not a problem as we don't have any. We're expecting a shipment sometime tomorrow."

The tall man stumbled and looked down. He had tripped against a young woman's arm. She moaned and turned over, and as she did so her hand fell open. Etched upon her palm, like a warning in some unknown calligraphy, was a six-pointed star.

"Oh, my God," said the man. He knelt by her and felt her forehead. Then he said to the nurse, "Have you got any aspirin?"

She looked at him in amazement. "You're joking. This woman is in group three—she's not expected to survive the night."

The man did not answer her. He held his hand to the young woman's cheek and whispered words in her ear. He sat back. "Kicsi," he said. "Kicsi, look up."

Kicsi opened her eyes. "I know you," she said in Hungarian. Her voice was so soft she could barely be heard. She shivered with fever. "But I can't know you, can I? You're the stranger."

"What did she say?" said the nurse.

"She said that she recognizes me."

"Are you a relative, then?"

"No, a—a friend. Her family gave me help and comfort when I needed it most. Come on—we have to carry her to the barracks. Can you give me a hand?"

"As I said before, she isn't expected—" The nurse stopped, staring at the blood-red star on the young woman's palm. "Oh, my God," she said. Since she had come to the camp she had seen nightmares. She had seen a man crawl out of a mass grave, had seen a group of rabbis perform a burial service over a pile of soap that had been made with human fat. She had seen a woman refuse food and starve herself to death in penance for the death of her daughter. Yet now this woman's star seemed to her to be the greatest horror of all, seemed to sum up everything that had gone before—something beyond understanding and yet unquestionably real. "Did they—did they do that to her?"

"No." The tall man bent over and picked up the young woman. Her bones were light as sticks. "I'm taking her to the barracks. She will survive. I swear it."

"Who are you?" said the nurse. She followed him, hurrying to catch up with him. "What are you?"

"She called me Vörös," said the man. "Redhead." He went into the dimly lit barracks and set Kicsi on a cot next to another woman. A few of the people on the other cots looked at them without curiosity. "How far is the nearest town?" he asked.

"The nearest—what on earth for?" said the nurse.

"To get some medicine. Aspirin at least. How far?"

"A few miles down the road."

"Thank you," said Vörös. "I'll be back after nightfall." He left the barracks, walking quickly. Within a few minutes he was lost among the afternoon shadows. The nurse shrugged and went back to her work.

The town was farther than the nurse had said, but Vörös made good time. He managed to hitch a ride on an army truck for the last few miles. They let him off near the center of the town.

Vörös stood for a while, eyes narrowed, studying the houses in the twilight. Then he made his choice. He walked up the steps to a well-kept white house and knocked on the door.

He heard the sound of someone walking up to the door, but the door did not open. "Who is it?" a woman said.

"I work at the camp a few miles down the road," Vörös said. "We need some medicine badly. Do you have anything? Aspirin, anything at all?"

The woman opened the door a crack. Vörös smiled and held out his hands to show that they were empty. "The camp?" she said.

"Yes. A lot of people have died, and we want to— we're trying to help—"

"I didn't know."

"What?"

"I said I didn't know," the woman repeated. She opened the door wider. Her hair was gray and black and she wore glasses. Her dress was as tidy as her house. "Those soldiers, they say that we should have done something. Something to help those people. Well, how could we? We only just found out about it. We didn't know what was happening."

"I don't care," said Vörös. His face was white against his red hair and beard. "I just want some medicine, that's all."

"And even if we did know, what could we have done? Jump in front of a train? Is that what you would have done, eh? Who are you, anyway? You're not one of those British."

"I want," Vörös said slowly, "some medicine. Anything. Please."

The woman looked at him closely. Then she seemed to make up her mind. "Just a minute." She turned and closed the door behind her.

A few minutes later the door opened again. "Here," she said, giving Vörös some aspirin. She hesitated for a while, and then said suddenly, "Good luck to you, traveler."

"Thank you," said Vörös. "The same to you." He went down the steps and headed toward the camp.

The sun had set by the time he got there. The nurse was gone, probably resting. He hurried to the barracks, to Kicsi. She was asleep. Her breath was shallow and her condition had not changed. Sweat pooled around her eyes, and her forehead was hot as flame. He opened her mouth and tried to make her swallow the aspirin. Then he gave some aspirin to the people who were awake and put the rest in his pocket. He breathed deeply, went outside, and sat down propped against a wall of the shelter. After a while he drew his coat around him and went to sleep.

The nurse came up to him the next morning as he opened his eyes. He stood and stretched.

"I don't know what you did to those people in there, but they seem to be doing much better," the nurse said, nodding toward the barracks. "I'm—I'm sorry if I seemed rude to you yesterday. I— There's a good deal on my mind."

"I understand," said Vörös. "How's Kicsi?"

"The young woman?" The nurse shrugged. "There's been

no change. But she's still alive. We didn't expect that much yesterday. How did it go in town?"

Vörös pulled the aspirin from his pocket. He rubbed his eyes with his free hand and started toward the barracks. "Not much, I'm afraid," he said.

The nurse nodded. "It's more than we've got," she said, following him. "The shipment of medicine didn't come through today. Apparently things are much worse than we first thought. Why— How could people do a thing like this?" She made a gesture that covered the camp.

"I don't know," Vörös said. He stopped, aware that she wanted something more from him. "I'm sorry."

"Well," she said. "There's a pot of tea in the shelter. It was still warm the last time I checked."

"Thank you," he said. "I'll be there later." He continued to the barracks.

Inside the barracks he blinked, adjusting his eyes to the dim light. He sat down by Kicsi and felt her forehead, speaking words to her as cool as a stream. She moaned and turned away. Someone behind him whispered, "It's him. Vörös," and he looked around.

Two girls stood in a narrow corridor between cots. One nudged the other and said, "Go on, tell him." Vörös smiled at them.

"I wanted to tell you," the other girl began. "My sister—she said she had seen you. She said you were going to take her away. She was a little crazy by then—we all were, I guess—and I thought the red-haired man was her name for death. She even sang a song about you. And then she —she disappeared. I thought she had died. But we just heard from the Red Cross—she's alive, she had been taken in by a family and lived in their cellar for a year. So—thank you. I don't know how you did it, but thank you."

Vörös nodded. "And," the girl went on, "well, I'm feeling better, and the nurse says my fever is down, so—" She stopped, then continued in a rush, "if you need a cot for that woman there so she can sleep by herself, well, she can have mine. If she's a friend of yours she can have it."

"Why, thank you," said Vörös. He looked pleased for the first time since he had come to the camp. He lifted Kicsi and carried her to the empty cot. "Thank you very much."

"I hope—I hope she gets better," the girl said, and went outside.

Vörös sat for a long time by the cot, his eyes half closed. Then he got up and went to check on the other patients, giving them the rest of the aspirin, soothing their fever with cool words. Once he stopped, smiled, and pulled a cigarette from his pocket. The man he was talking to accepted it thankfully. A long time later he went to the shelter for some food.

The nurse was there, talking to a few soldiers. As Vörös came in, she turned and went up to him. "Hello," she said. "How've you been?"

Vörös shrugged. "Busy," he said, helping himself to tea.

"The patients seem to think you're some kind of miracle worker," the nurse said. "Quite a lot of them have recovered faster than I'd looked for. And they tell stories about you, and there's a song—I'm sure you've heard it." Vörös shrugged. "You know, it's odd. Sometimes I believe them. After all, if nightmares are real, then miracles should be too."

She poured herself some tea. "There's still no change in your young friend, is there?"

"No," said Vörös.

"Well . . ." said the nurse. She sighed. "Sometimes it takes time."

Vörös worked all through the next few days. The cots emptied as the patients got well or fell into fever dreams from which they never recovered. Once as Vörös passed his hand over Kicsi's forehead she looked up at him. Her eyes were fever-blind and bright as mirrors. She said nothing, and her eyes closed again wearily.

"I think the fever is about to break," Vörös said to the nurse.

"I hope so," the nurse said. "I didn't want to bring this up before, but—well, we'll probably be leaving here soon, going to places where they'll need us more. If she isn't well by then—I don't know. Can you take care of her?"

Vörös nodded, his face drawn.

The fever broke the next day. Kicsi opened her eyes slowly and looked around her. A patient in the cot next to her was being fed with care by one of the nurses. I don't understand, she thought. Why are they feeding us if they tried to kill us? And at the back of her mind she thought,

I can't stay here—I have to go to work. But she felt so tired. She rolled over and went to sleep.

When she woke again she saw Vörös sitting next to her. At first she did not recognize him: his place was in the forest and the houses of her old village, not the barracks in which she had spent the last year of her life. She could only connect him with the song they had sung in the camps: *"When you're doing all you can,/You'll see him come . . ."* And he had come to her. She was puzzled. She felt that she should know him.

"Hello, Kicsi," said the red-haired man softly. "When you talked about traveling to faraway places this was not what you had in mind, was it?"

Who was he? How did he know her name? The effort of concentrating on what he was saying was too much. She stared at the ceiling. She wished he would go away.

"I'm sorry," the man went on. She could barely hear him. "I should not have joked with you so soon. You want rest, and food."

She could not turn to look at him. Later, though she could not tell how much later, she heard him say, "What? I don't understand." There was pain in his voice, but she did not know why.

"Were—did she lose many relatives?" she heard a nurse say.

"Relatives? I don't know. At least her parents, I think, and I haven't been able to find her brother or her sisters."

"That's it then. She feels guilty for living when so many have died," said the nurse. "And she feels disoriented as well. She doesn't know where she is. She may not even know who you are. She's just recovering from typhus, remember."

"Guilty . . ." he said. "I've seen it too, of course, but I never thought that it would happen to her."

The nurse shrugged.

"What happens?" he said. "What can I do?"

"What happens?" said the nurse. "Well, sometimes they die. Sometimes they return to life, though. Remember, these are the survivors."

"Well," said Vörös. "Is she well enough to eat, do you think?"

By the time he came back with a bowl and spoon Kicsi had remembered his name, who he was. He seemed as unimportant as a character in a forgotten dream, someone connected with a life that was now gone. She could not understand what he was doing in the barracks. She thought of the village, of the people who had gone and would not be coming back, but she could not feel anything for her old life. She remembered struggling to stay alive in the camp, but she could not remember why. They were liberated, but the world was still the same.

Vörös nursed Kicsi for several days. Almost everyone else had left. Slowly she began to realize what she had lost. One day she turned to him and said, "Dead." Her eyes were as dull as old silver.

"What?" said Vörös.

"Dead. They're all dead. Do you remember what he said, the village no-good? He said that they were all dead. And he was right."

"The village no-good?" said Vörös. "I haven't heard about him. Tell me."

She ignored him. "Everyone died. Everyone. Except me."

"Oh, Kicsi. Not everyone. There are hundreds of people, thousands, still alive. I've seen them, I've helped some of them . . ."

"Everyone. My mother and father. My sisters. Aladár."

"How do you know? They may still be alive."

"I know. I'm a witch." Kicsi held up her palm and showed him the mark. The scar had faded to bone white. "See? They said that I'm a witch and I am. I don't want to live anymore."

"Kicsi, please, you can't— I don't know what to do with you. Do you want to hear a story?"

The nurse came in and sat on the cot beside Vörös. "How—how is she?"

"She doesn't want to live," Vörös said. "She doesn't care anymore." He sighed. "I don't know what hurts me more— what she says to me or the dead tone in which she says it."

"I suppose you have to find a way to make her want to live."

"I know," said Vörös. "I don't know how."

The nurse looked at him, puzzled. "I thought you knew her."

"I did—I don't—I knew her family. I told her stories of faraway places."

"Tell her some more."

"I thought of that, but—well—don't you think she's seen enough of life outside her village? Once she couldn't wait to leave, and now she would go back if she had any chance at all."

"Where do you think she wants to go?" said the nurse.

Vörös asked Kicsi the nurse's question. Kicsi said nothing. "I don't know," he said.

"The reason I asked—well, we've been given our orders. We leave tomorrow. Everyone who's not well or who has no place to go will be sent to a Displaced Persons camp, but I can't guarantee what it'll be like there. You might want to take her with you, to your—your home. Where are you from?"

"Nowhere," said Vörös. "I have no home."

"Oh," said the nurse. She sounded very tired, defeated. "Well, then. I just don't know what to do. Can you take her with you? I think she'll fare better with you than in an institution."

"Of course," said Vörös.

"Well then," said the nurse. "I'll say good-bye to you now. I don't expect to see you tomorrow, what with all the fuss. Good-bye—and thanks."

All the next day they heard the sound of jeeps and trucks as the soldiers came and tore down their temporary buildings. Patients who were leaving for the Displaced Persons camp came to say good-bye to Vörös. A few of them wept. "I'll never forget you," one said. "You saved my life."

Vörös went outside the barracks as the last of the patients left. "You there! Red!" called one of the soldiers. "Give us a hand here, would you?"

Vörös nodded. He walked over to the temporary shelter and carried the pieces of wood they handed him to the truck. For the next few hours Kicsi was left alone. She heard nothing but the sound of nails tearing from wood, boards knocking together, soldiers cursing, trucks rumbling down the dirt road. The men sitting at the back of the trucks called to Vörös as they left, and then everything was silent.

Vörös came into the barracks and sat down on the cot next to Kicsi. "Well," he said. "I guess we're the only ones left. And this time, I swear it, I will make you interested in life again. I didn't pull you back from the dead for this."

The walls of the barracks blew away suddenly, and the roof spun off into the sky. Kicsi gasped. Vörös took her hand and raised her up off the cot, higher, higher, until the cots, the camp, the countryside, dwindled to something she could hold in her hand.

"See, Kicsi. That is Europe," said Vörös. "It's true that many people died. I can't lie to you." As he spoke she could see columns of smoke rising up toward them—black smoke, clogged with the smell of death. Fires burned unchecked across the land. She heard people crying in pain, hungry and hurt, filling the earth with their tears, and far away, on the edges of the world, she heard the sea calling back to them.

"But the wounds will heal, Kicsi. See, the land revives. And the people—already the people are finding new ways of life, learning to live again." She saw a tracery of green spread across the land, a slow stain of healing. People greeted relatives thought to be dead, rejoiced, moved in a great stream away from the burned lands, out toward the new lands of Palestine or America. "That is how it has always been. And underneath it, though you do not see it, though you will not believe me, is a kind of joy. The joy of life."

They began to move above the world, seeing what it had become. In places the war was still being fought; in other places the soldiers were beginning to come home. They saw movement everywhere. Vörös showed her stone castles and tall cathedrals, lakes and forests and walls of mountains.

Then they moved faster. Kicsi understood that they traveled away from Europe now, over the Mediterranean, over vast deserts holding heat. The world sped by them in a blur—statues of stone and great palaces of ivory, ruined temples, arches and columns and long broken stretches of roadways. They saw cities standing by great rivers that flashed green as they passed, small towns nearly covered by trees, isolated houses far from comfort. Sometimes Kicsi saw something that she thought she recognized: the Himalayas, the Taj Mahal, the Great Wall of China. And then they were speeding across another ocean, this one almost unbelievably vast, over toward America.

They had nearly crossed America before Kicsi realized

where she was. Another ocean shone like metal before them, and she saw New York, its tall buildings standing guard on the edge of the continent. Then they were over the water, moving toward Europe again, and toward their starting point.

"What did you think?" said Vörös. "How did you like the world? You see, you got your wish—the one you wished that day a long time ago—that you would see far-away places."

"I—I don't know," said Kicsi slowly. "You know, I don't think I'll ever enjoy anything again."

"Well, then," said Vörös. "I'm going to have to try again."

Kicsi looked down. For a moment she thought she was back at the village. But it was smaller than the village, and less important—just a crossroads and a few houses. The forest was larger, the distance to the next village greater. She understood that she was seeing the village as it had been hundreds and hundreds of years ago.

As she watched, settlers came to the village on horses. More houses went up. A thriving market grew by the cross-roads. Trees were felled for their wood. The synagogue was built and the graveyard consecrated.

Vörös showed Kicsi two people, a young man and woman. She watched as they built a house for themselves with the help of their friends and as they blessed it and settled in. She saw the man go to till the fields every day and the woman stay at home and take care of the new house they had built. She saw the man come home in the evening, and she saw the two of them embrace and eat by firelight the dinner that the woman had prepared.

Then the woman became ill. The man stopped going to the fields and stayed at home, helplessly watching the house decay as the woman sank into her fever. He sent for a rabbi from the neighboring town, as the small village did not yet have its own rabbi. He changed the woman's name, in the hope that the Angel of Death would become confused and return to heaven without the woman's soul. He prayed. He did not eat. He sat staring into the firelight for hours, until it seemed to Kicsi that everything in the room became tinged with the red wash of fire.

He did not seem surprised when, one day, he looked up and saw the Angel of Death standing over the woman.

"Please," he said. "Do not take her yet."

"I must take her," said the angel. "It is written."

"No," said the man. "Take me in her place."

The angel seemed to consider this, but finally he said, "No. I want this soul, and not yours. Not yet."

The man became angry. "If you take her," he said, "I will end my life. I will throw myself into the fire, to follow her."

"You cannot do that," said the angel. "I do not want your soul. If you do that, you will doom yourself to wander the earth until the end, until the Messiah comes. You will never see her again."

"I do not believe you," said the man. "It is a trick to prevent me from following her."

"As you wish," said the angel, and he gathered up the woman's soul and took it away with him, but the man did not see where they went. He threw himself into the fire, and was burned.

Then it seemed to Kicsi that she could see the man's soul moving from place to place in the village, unhappy, restless, unable to find peace. He began to frighten travelers who came to the village—Kicsi remembered a story István had once told, of a spirit that lived in the woods—but after a hundred years had passed he stopped.

Kicsi turned to Vörös. "I know why you showed me that," she said. "You want to tell me that I shouldn't throw away my life because someone else has died."

"I had that in mind, yes," said Vörös. "But that was not why I showed you the man. You see, I know him."

Kicsi said nothing. "Ah, Kicsi," said Vörös. "I remember a time when you would have wondered at that."

"I'm not a young child anymore," said Kicsi.

"Yes, you are," said Vörös. "You are very young." He called to the spirit in the village, and it came to meet them. It looked very much like the young man she had seen, but when she looked at it directly it seemed to fade, to grow transparent.

"This young woman does not wish to live," Vörös said to the spirit. "What would you show her?"

"The old things," said the spirit. Its voice sounded like wind speaking to old ruined houses.

"Which ones?" said Vörös.

"Egypt," said the spirit. "Jerusalem."

"Show us," said Vörös.

They were over Egypt now, watching as workers built the great pyramids, carrying blocks of newly cut stone across the miles, sweating under the hot sun. Kicsi thought of Imre, in the haze of the candlelight, saying, "We were slaves in the land of Egypt. . . ." She turned away.

"No," said Vörös. His voice seemed to come from far away. "I don't think we should be showing her this. It reminds her too much of what she has been through."

"Yes," said the spirit.

She looked down and saw the walled city of Jerusalem as it was hundreds of years ago. People in many-colored costumes walked quickly through the narrow cobbled streets. Others asked for admittance at the gates, and were passed through. She saw men with fine robes and bright rings on their fingers bring their tribute to the city—elephants, camels, peacocks. Craftsmen called by the king came from all over to design the temple, bringing with them the richest grains of wood in their lands.

Vörös looked at Kicsi. "What do you think?"

"I don't know," she said. "I think I remember a time when I would have wanted to see this, but it seems so long ago now."

"I don't know," said Vörös. "I don't know what to do with you. There is nothing left to show you."

"Nothing," said the spirit, "save the spirit world."

The world changed slightly. Below them she could still see Jerusalem on the hill, but the air was thickening about them. A winged shape, black and covered with scales, flew past them. Another shape, seemingly made of fire, burned across the sky. Something white drifted toward them, and as it came closer Kicsi saw that it was a woman with white staring eyes. Far off she heard something moan in torment. Kicsi understood that she was seeing demons and angels on their own errands. She drew closer to Vörös.

"Over there," said the spirit suddenly. Vörös looked to where he was pointing. Quickly Vörös said a word over Kicsi and moved her behind him. A woman flew close to them, a woman with a white face and night-black hair that flew out behind her like a cloak. Her lips were blood red and her teeth were pointed.

"That was Lilith," said Vörös. "The child-stealer."

The sky darkened. Points of light trailed past them—

shining eyes or teeth or nails. In the distance a skull flashed against the sky like a comet, and was gone. The lights began to draw closer to them, seeking them, hunting them.

"Come," said Vörös. "Quickly." The night grew darker. There were no stars. To the east Kicsi could see a faint light, and she wondered how the dawn could be coming so soon after nightfall. It was toward the light that Vörös led them.

The night spirits hurried after them. They called to Vörös, asking him to stop, to turn back. A great silken net loomed up in front of Kicsi, and she broke through it, trailing delicate weblike strands. She shuddered.

She heard her name, and looked back. The spirits called to her, promising her rest. A child on a silver horse sang to her, telling her of the peace of death. Come with us, they called. Leave your grief with the living and follow us. There is rest here.

She slowed. Ahead of her she saw Vörös and the spirit flying toward the eastern light, their arms outstretched. Come with me, sang the child, washed in the light of the silver horse. All those you knew are dead. Find rest with me.

Vörös saw her then. One minute he was far away, nearly lost in the distance, and the next he was by her side, with the spirit beside him. A look of horror was on his face. "Go back!" he said to the spirits. He called to them by their names. "Go back and follow us no more." He grasped Kicsi by her wrist and pulled her toward the light.

The night demons slowed, turned away, calling to each other with shrill voices. Then they were gone.

Vörös stopped. Below them Kicsi saw an angel. His face was made of light and in his hands he held a spiral sword.

"He is one of the four angels who stand watch over the Garden of Eden," said Vörös. "The demons cannot abide his light. We are safe as long as we stay here. How are you feeling?"

"I don't know," said Kicsi. "Tired."

"Shall we go back?"

"I don't care," said Kicsi.

Vörös sighed. "Come, then," he said.

"You are going into realms where I cannot follow," said the spirit. "Good-bye."

"Good-bye," said Vörös.

Below them Kicsi saw the outline of Europe reappear, clouded with smoke. They drifted awhile, looking at the people below them. "It was all illusion, you know," said Vörös. "You were never in any danger."

"Oh," said Kicsi.

"You do want to die, then," said Vörös.

She said nothing.

"You look tired," said Vörös. Then suddenly: "Wait," he said.

"What is it?" said Kicsi. They had stopped.

"Nothing," said Vörös. "I thought I saw—yes, it was him. Over there. Come this way."

They fell back to earth slowly, toward an emergency station that had been set up by the Red Cross. No one seemed to notice them. As they came closer Kicsi could see that lists had been posted—the lists of the names of the dead. Standing in front of one of the lists was a man. His gray-black hair was longer, wilder, and his gray eyes were fiercer, but she knew him. It was the rabbi.

She saw him read his daughter's name from the lists of the dead. "I will get revenge," she heard him say. "I will find that traveler—the man who spoke the words of evil omen at my daughter's wedding—and I will kill him. I will have my revenge."

And then she and Vörös were back inside the barracks, on the cot, as though nothing had happened.

Chapter

8

Vörös sat with his head in his hand, looking at the wall, saying nothing. Finally Kicsi said, "He can't really kill you, can he?"

Vörös turned to her and laughed. "Why do you say that? Certainly he can."

"But—" She remembered another time, long ago, when the rabbi had threatened to kill Vörös. She remembered her fear then, the horrible certainty that Vörös would die. She did not feel afraid now. Perhaps, she thought, too many people had died. Perhaps she would never be afraid of death again. "But he said he would kill you if he saw you in the village."

"He said that he would kill me if his daughter was harmed."

"Oh. But he can't really believe—I mean, it wasn't you that—"

"No," said Vörös. "But he thinks it was. His mind has been twisted by the war, and by all the deaths. His village, his congregation, is gone. I'm afraid he sees all his enemies as equals. I am the same as the Germans who killed his daughter, in his eyes."

"Oh," Kicsi said again. "But he can't really harm you,

can he? Last time, when he tried, you escaped, remember? Your magic is stronger than his."

"Kicsi," said Vörös, "let me tell you something. His magic is stronger than mine and always has been. Last time, when I escaped, it was by luck, and with the aid of a friend." He looked at the far wall again and said nothing for a long time.

"Well," said Kicsi, "what will happen now? Are we going to die?"

"We may," said Vörös. "I am very weary. I have worked the last three years without stopping. I will need my pack to continue."

"Your pack," said Kicsi. "I have it. I hid it in the walls—"

"I know," said Vörös. "I have been back once to find it, but the house was filled with soldiers."

"Soldiers? In our house?"

"Yes. It was then that I knew that you and your family had been taken. I would have come back sooner but I had pressing errands . . ."

"Soldiers," said Kicsi. "In our house. Who lives there now, I wonder?"

"I would like to find out. If I can get back my pack I might be able to stand against the rabbi. Will you come with me, back to your village? It will be painful for you, I know."

"I have nowhere else to go," said Kicsi. "I may as well come with you. What do we do now? Do you snap your fingers and we return to the village?"

"Kicsi," said Vörös. "You have not been listening to me. I have no magic left. We must walk, and ride the trains."

"No magic?" said Kicsi. "But—what about the trip we just took? Around the world, and to Jerusalem—"

"That was illusion. None of it was real. I put on a show for you, to see if you would come alive again. You did not." Suddenly Vörös sounded very old. "But illusion will never work against the rabbi. He is too clever for that. So. Do you still want to come with me? I have nothing else to offer you. Very possibly, it will be dangerous."

"I will come," Kicsi said. "I am not afraid of death anymore."

She spent the next few days resting and gathering strength. Vörös went into the town several times for food and supplies. Gradually she was able to eat a whole meal, to walk about the camp. Life seemed unreal without the barking of dogs and the roaring of the furnaces. She felt that she had seen beneath the mask of the world, and she could not quite believe in that mask again.

One day after Vörös came back from the town he said, "It has been eighteen days since I first came to this camp. Eighteen is the number of *chai*, the Hebrew word for life. It would be good to leave now. Do you think you are ready?"

"Yes."

Vörös looked at her carefully. "Do not be so willing to throw your life away. The rabbi is after us, as I thought. If you see anything at all unusual, I want you to tell me. Can you do that?"

"Yes," she said again.

Vörös shrugged. "All right then," he said. "Let's go."

They left the camp quickly, without looking back, and began to walk along the road to the train station. The road was hot and dusty and they rested often. Occasionally they passed soldiers on leave or refugees traveling in groups carrying all their possessions between them. No one stopped to look at them, the tall man in the long black coat and the pale young woman in the new town-bought dress and shoes.

Kicsi thought that none of it could be real—not the people, or the well-kept houses, or the trees and shrubs flowering by the roadside. Sometimes, when she passed a soldier, she marveled that there could be anyone so healthy left in the world. Sometimes she would finger the cloth of her dress, wondering at its newness. She and Vörös did not speak.

The train station was small and very crowded. Soldiers were allowed on the trains first, and several trains passed before Kicsi and Vörös found spaces. As they climbed on board Vörös said, "Are you hungry?"

"Yes," said Kicsi.

"Why didn't you say something to me?"

"I don't know."

They sat down next to a soldier. As the train started, Vörös asked him if he could spare some food. He rummaged in his pack and found some chocolate. "Where are you people going?" the soldier asked. Kicsi looked out the window.

Vörös gave him the name of Kicsi's village.

"I've heard of it," the soldier said, his eyes narrowing in puzzlement. "I talked to someone who was in the fighting there, if it's the place I'm thinking of. A strange town. Odd things happening there, especially at night."

Vörös leaned forward. "What things?" he said.

"I can't remember. He was glad to leave—I can remember that." The soldier looked at Vörös with a new curiosity. "Why do you want to go there."

"I left something of mine there," Vörös said. "Before the war. I'd like to see if it's still there."

"It'd better be something important," said the soldier. "You wouldn't catch me going to that town. I still remember the way this fellow looked. And what he said—that the lamps aren't lit at night. And something about—about wolves. . . ." He looked at Vörös as if asking him a question.

Vörös shrugged. "I don't know," he said.

The train stopped nearly an hour later. "Come," Vörös said to Kicsi. "We change trains here." He nodded to the soldier as they left the train.

Another train was pulling out of the station as they descended. A voice over the public address system called out destinations, arrivals, train numbers. Vörös took Kicsi's hand and led her to a row of benches. "Sit there for a minute," he said. "I have to see about tickets."

She sat on the hard wooden bench and looked around her. The station was not out in the open like the last one, but enclosed inside a large building. Voices and the sounds of trains starting and stopping echoed off the distant walls and ceiling. People walked by her, talking in half a dozen languages, hurrying to catch their trains.

Vörös came back. "Our train leaves in another hour," he said. "We won't have any problems getting on. Everyone wants to go west, and not east." Suddenly he stopped and stood up.

"It is them, it is!" Kicsi heard someone say. People were running toward them, hugging Kicsi, holding her as though afraid to let her go. Someone was crying.

Kicsi stepped back. Tibor and Ilona stood before her. She felt confused. Would the dead start coming to life now? Or was this another illusion? "Hello," she said slowly.

"Kicsi!" said Ilona. "Are you all right? How are you? Where have you been?"

"I—I'm fine," said Kicsi. She backed away. There were too many people around her; she was not used to talking.

"Vörös, what's wrong with her?" said Tibor. "Doesn't she recognize us?"

"She recognizes you," said Vörös. "Come, we're very hungry. Let's find some food, and I'll tell you about it."

They made their way to a small market near the station. "We met someone who said he had seen you at the camp after you were liberated," Ilona said to Kicsi as Vörös picked out fruit, cheese, bread, "so we knew you were still alive. Tibor and I met at a Red Cross station—we had been in the same camp for a while but had never seen each other. We decided we had to find you. We've been in the station two days, trying to get to where the man said he saw you. There just aren't any tickets. We slept on the benches—that's why our clothes are so dirty." Ilona had stopped crying. She took a deep breath and went on. "The Red Cross says—they say everyone else died. In the family, I mean. The Red Cross has lists, you know." She stopped and looked at Kicsi carefully. "Are you all right?"

They sat down by the station and began to eat. "I'm all right," said Kicsi. "A little tired."

"Did you know someone named Aladár?" said Vörös. "She thinks he is dead."

"Ali," said Ilona. "Yes, he is. We just found out. What—what can we do for her?"

"I don't know," said Vörös, biting into an apple. "What did you have in mind when you searched for her?"

"We—Tibor and I—we were going to go to a Displaced Persons camp. And then, well, they send people away, to different countries. America, Canada. I don't know. It sounded good to us. Do you think she would like to come with us?"

"I don't know," said Vörös. "Why not ask her?"

"Oh—oh, of course," said Ilona. "I don't know why— Kicsi, what do you think? Do you think you would like to come with us?"

"No," said Kicsi.

"No?" said Tibor. "But why not? Where are you going?"

"Back to the village," said Kicsi. "With Vörös."

"Kicsi, that was before you had somewhere else to go," said Vörös.

"Back to the village?" said Ilona, interrupting. "But why?"

"I have to go with Vörös," said Kicsi. "He has something to do there."

"No, you are not coming with me," said Vörös. "I only took you with me because you had no place else to go. It's too dangerous. You are going with your family."

"No," said Kicsi. "I am not."

"Why—why do you want to go with him?" Ilona asked, but Kicsi did not look up from her food.

Later Vörös turned to Ilona and said softly, "It will be a very dangerous journey. She thinks she will die if she goes. She does not think it is fair that Aladár should die and she should live. I think she wants to do something heroic, like Aladár."

"Oh," said Ilona. "Well, she's not going with you. She's coming with us."

"I would hope so," said Vörös. "But she is very stubborn. If she goes with you she may find some way to kill herself. Perhaps I should take her with me, as I originally planned. I will try to keep her safe."

"If she goes with you," said Ilona, "then I am coming too."

"Ilona," said Vörös. "You don't know what you are saying. Someone is trying to kill me. He will kill you too, if you get in his way. And you will only make it more dangerous for me, if you come along. I will be responsible for your safety as well as for Kicsi's."

"We're the last of the family," said Ilona. "We're responsible for each other. And—well—you don't know what it's like, being alone, thinking you're the last one alive of all your family." Vörös said nothing. "I can't leave my sister now that I've found her. I'm coming along. It's settled."

"What's settled?" said Tibor.

"I'm going back to the village with Vörös and Kicsi," said Ilona. She looked at her sister. Kicsi did not seem to have heard anything.

"This is crazy!" said Tibor. "You can't be serious. Vörös said that it would be dangerous, isn't that right?" Vörös nodded slightly. "This is insane. We are the only ones left of our family and you want to get yourselves killed."

"Listen to him, Ilona," said Vörös. "Please."

"And what if something happens to Kicsi when I'm gone?" said Ilona.

"All right," said Tibor. "All right. I can't believe that you would willingly go into danger like this, but I am part of the family too. I'll have to go with you."

"Listen to me, all of you," said Vörös. His voice was very quiet. "A man is following me. He is trying to kill me. I have to get back to the village without him seeing me. How safe do you think I'd be traveling with a group of young people who seem to think that this whole thing is a family picnic?"

"But that's just it," said Ilona. "He probably thinks you're traveling alone. He'll never think to look for you in a group of people."

Vörös laughed suddenly. "You know, you might be right. My only hope lies in doing something he would not expect."

"Then we can come?" said Ilona.

"I don't know. I can't very well throw you off the train. I might have known you'd be as stubborn as your sister." Then he became serious. "But listen to me. I wasn't joking about the danger. You will see things—well, things you will not understand. Are you still willing to come along?"

"Yes," said Ilona, and Tibor shrugged.

"I have no choice, do I?" he said finally.

"All right, then," said Vörös. "Let's find a place to stay for the night."

They found lodgings at a small place near the station. Ilona and Kicsi took the bed and Tibor stretched out on the floor. Vörös leaned against the wall near the door.

Kicsi did not sleep well. Several times during the night she was startled awake by a dream or a noise. Each time she woke she saw Vörös sitting by the door, his eyes open. Once she thought she heard wolves howling in the distance. Vörös nodded at her, quietly, and she turned over and went to sleep.

"I don't like it," Vörös said in the morning. "I think he's found us."

"He's here?" said Tibor. "What can we do?"

"We can leave as quickly as possible," said Vörös.

After breakfast they boarded the train. At first Ilona

and Tibor watched silently as the miles of fields and forests passed by on either side of them, or talked in low voices among themselves, or shared a loaf of bread between them. Once Ilona turned to Kicsi and said, "Are you looking forward to going back to the village?"

"I don't know," said Kicsi.

Later Ilona said to her, "Was it bad where you were?"

"As bad as any other place, I guess," said Kicsi, and turned away.

After a few hours Tibor stood and began to walk to the end of the car.

"Where are you going?" said Vörös.

"I thought I'd look around a bit," said Tibor. "See what the other cars are like."

"No," said Vörös.

"Why—why not?"

"As long as we travel together I want everyone to stay with me," said Vörös. "I am responsible for all of us."

"Oh, but—" said Tibor. "Do you think he's on the train? I mean, wouldn't you have seen him get on?"

"Maybe," said Vörös. "Maybe not."

"You mean—he might be in disguise?"

"Something like that."

"Oh," said Tibor. He sat back down next to Ilona. "I was prepared for danger," he said to her, "but I don't know how much more of this boredom I can take." She laughed.

"Who is this man we're supposed to avoid, anyway?" said Tibor. "And what has Vörös done to him that he wants to kill him?"

"I don't know," said Ilona. "I think Kicsi knows, though. Those two have always had their secrets. But I wouldn't try asking her."

"No."

In the evening they came to another small town. They left the train and walked through the town, coming finally to a narrow side street and a small inn serving dinner. They were greeted at the door by a small fat man, a Czech.

"Well, what can I do for you?" said the man. "Food and then a room, is that it, sir?"

"Yes, thank you," said Vörös.

"Very good, very good," said the man, hurrying to the

table to seat Kicsi and Ilona. "Just sit over here and I'll be right back."

"Vörös," Tibor said as he sat down. "How much longer before we get to the village?"

"That depends," said Vörös. "I think there's a stretch of railway around here that's been bombed, and if it is we'll have to take a longer way. We may even have to walk for a few miles."

"And if the railways have been fixed?"

"If the railways have been fixed, and if the man who is hunting me does not find me, we will be in the village in a few days."

"Good," said Tibor. "What's it like now, the village?"

"Changed," said Vörös. "Like every other town in Europe." The fat man came back and poured each of them a glass of wine. Vörös took a sip and went on. "There are parts of the village you would not recognize. And there are places that have been changed only slightly. Those will be the hardest for you to bear, I think."

"What do you mean?" said Ilona. "Which places?"

But Vörös was not listening. His eyes had narrowed and he was watching carefully some people who had just come through the door.

Tibor and Ilona looked at the door. Imre and Sarah stood there, their arms outstretched. Imre held his left arm awkwardly, as he had always done.

"Mother!" said Ilona joyfully. She and Tibor stood, pushing back their chairs.

"No!" said Vörös. He waited a moment, then said a short word sharp as a blade and threw his wineglass at the two by the door. The glass passed through them and shattered against the wall. Someone screamed. Wine trickled slowly to the floor. Imre and Sarah wavered, then vanished as slowly as smoke.

The other patrons turned to look at Vörös, or at the wineglass, or to talk loudly among themselves. The small fat man hurried toward Vörös. "I'm sorry," said Vörös. "I will pay for the damages. Do you need help cleaning up?"

"I don't— What happened? Who were those people? I thought—I thought I saw them disappear . . ."

Vörös shrugged and said nothing.

"Why did you have to throw your glass at them?" the man said.

Ilona began to cry. She cried as she had always done, with her hands over her mouth instead of her eyes, as though it was her mouth that would give her away. "I didn't know," she said finally. The fat man looked around the table, shrugged, and went to clear away the broken glass. "I thought—I thought I could survive anything, because—because of what I'd been through. But I didn't know it would be like this. I know you warned us, but I thought—I don't know—" She began to cry again. "Who is he? Who do you know that would do—would do—something like that?"

"You know him," said Vörös. "The rabbi."

"The *rabbi?*" said Tibor. He held on to his wineglass to steady his hands. "He wouldn't—I know him. He taught me my bar mitzvah lesson. And he prayed for my father—" He stopped.

"Try not to think about it," said Vörös.

Tibor nodded.

"It's true, then," said Ilona. "You can work magic. And so can the rabbi. I always thought that Kicsi was imagining things . . ." She looked at her sister, who sat staring straight ahead as though nothing had happened. "But why? Why is he after you?"

Vörös told her. "But he knows now that I am traveling with you. He must know or he would not have called up that illusion. I don't know what he hoped to do. Maybe he just wanted to frighten you away. Maybe he wanted you to follow the illusion and so get to me through you. I don't know. As I said, he is not in his right mind."

Ilona let out a shaky breath. "You were right," she said. "We are a danger to you. Especially now that he knows we are here. I guess—I guess we should go back. Back to the DP camp. What do you think, Tibor?"

"I don't know," said Tibor. "I still can't believe it. That the rabbi . . . How did he survive the war?"

"In the shape of a wolf," said Vörös.

"In the shape of—" said Tibor. He laughed softly. "It sounds so reasonable when you say it. I can almost believe it. Did you know he was going to do . . . what he did?"

"I knew he was going to do something," said Vörös. "He is a master of illusion. Do you remember when I first saw you, at the train station?" Tibor nodded. "I hesitated before going up to you because I feared that you might be an illusion."

The fat man brought them trays of hot meat and vegetables. He served them silently. The other patrons had gone back to their dinners.

After a little while Vörös said, "What do you plan to do now?"

"I thought we might—I mean—" Tibor stopped, put his head in his hands. "Ohhhh," he said, a long whispery sigh that shuddered with every heartbeat. "I don't know. I just don't know. What can we do?"

Vörös looked at him carefully. "Tibor," he said. "Your father was a very wise man. But you cannot acquire his wisdom by pretending to have it already."

Tibor nodded slowly. "Can I think about it?" he said. "I'll tell you in the morning."

The fat man came to their table and began to clear it away. Without looking at them he said, "You cannot stay here tonight. I'm sorry. The other patrons think that you're—well, that you're sorcerers."

"That's ridiculous," said Tibor. "Do we look like sorcerers to you?" He made a gesture that took in everyone at the table, daring the fat man to look at Kicsi, who was staring blindly in front of her, at Ilona, her eyes still red from crying, at Vörös.

"Tibor," said Vörös gently. Then to the fat man he said, "That's all right. We'll be leaving soon."

"Thank you, sir," said the man. He bowed as he took the dishes away.

"Where will we go?" said Ilona. "It's too late to find another place—"

"Where?" said Vörös. "To the forest."

They finished the wine and left the lighted inn. The road was very dark and the stars were cold and far away, comfortless. Kicsi felt small and lost, like a ghost walking among ghosts. Somewhere, she knew, a fifth ghost waited without pity, waited to kill them all. It did not seem important.

They entered the forest one at a time, walking slowly. Vörös gathered together some logs and twigs and started a fire. They arranged themselves in front of it and went to sleep.

That night the howling of wolves was closer than before.

Kicsi woke once to see Vörös sitting in front of the fire, feeding it twigs and bits of leaves. Tiny sparks cracked out of the fire's heart and reflected in his eyes, gold within blue. She lay down and went back to sleep.

They woke the next morning and stretched, easing the soreness out of their joints. Tibor walked over to Vörös.

"I've talked it over with Ilona," Tibor said. "We've decided—well, we want to go back. To the DP camp in Italy. We're no good to you here. We'd like Kicsi to come with us, of course, but we don't think she would."

"No," said Vörös. "She wouldn't." They both looked at Kicsi, who sat staring into the dying fire. The forest was very quiet.

"Well," said Tibor. "You'll take care of her, won't you? And when this whole thing is over, will you bring her back to us?"

"I'll try," said Vörös.

"You know," said Tibor, "I couldn't sleep last night. I kept thinking—they weren't dreams, they were very real— I kept seeing the way our parents looked. And I kept wondering what he would try to do next. What if the next illusion is—is Aladár?"

"I know," said Vörös. "I've thought of that myself. I don't know."

They left the forest and came, tired and hungry, to the train station. Vörös bought a few loaves of bread for the trip and gave one each to Ilona and Tibor. People who had been at the inn the night before avoided them, and once they heard the word *sorcerer*.

"Good-bye," said Ilona. She embraced Kicsi and whispered to her, "Are you sure you don't want to come with us?"

"I'm sure," said Kicsi.

"Be careful," said Ilona. She stepped back and smoothed her sister's hair. "Come back to us."

Kicsi said nothing.

"Good-bye," said Tibor, and they turned to board their train.

The train Vörös and Kicsi were to take came soon afterward. They boarded and sat down, not speaking. The train pulled away from the station. Vörös, sitting near the window, watched the fields of grain pass.

Suddenly he turned to Kicsi. "I would like to tell you a story," he said. "Would you like to hear it?"

Kicsi shrugged. "I don't care."

"All right," said Vörös. "This time it will be a true story. You will know that it is true because you are in it—part of it. It is the story of a part of my life. You know—I have told you—that it is dangerous for me to speak of myself, that words are weapons and it is safest to say nothing at all. But I feel I must tell you this—that I must explain."

Kicsi nodded once, slightly.

"The story starts before I met you and your family. You see, it was given to me to see the future—not all the future, but that part of it that would happen during the war. Night and day I saw before me smoke and furnaces and barbed wire. Night and day I heard the cries of those who were beaten and starved and tortured. I knew that I was given this sight so that I could help as many as I could. But, you see, no one else saw the things I did. No one else had my urgency. And I did not know when these things would take place—if they were in the past or in the future or only in my imagination. I think I went a little crazy, like your rabbi is now. 'You must leave!' I said to everyone I met. 'Death is coming!' And they all looked at me as though I had lost my wits. They could not see death. They did not understand why I acted the way I did.

"Anyway, that's why I began to make mistakes. The first was when I talked of death at the wedding of the rabbi's daughter. When that woman began to cry I knew that her son was dead. I could see him as the flames took him, could see him clearer than I could see the wedding canopy in front of me. But I should not have said so at the wedding. I was driven by what I saw.

"I made my second mistake shortly after that, in the forest. I should not have shown the rabbi the word I had written on the golem's forehead. Had I been thinking clearly I would have known that. But I saw the man with no teeth in front of me, and I could not tell when he would come. I only knew that the village must be protected from him."

Vörös paused for a moment, then continued. "For this mistake I paid with the life of one of my closest friends. He was a magician too, Akan was. We had traveled much together, studying ancient tapestries and pieces of parchment, looking in far-off cities for books of old spells, buying dusty amulets in remote bazaars. He was a subtle magician, and his knowledge was great. I should be dead by now, but for him."

"I know what you mean," said Kicsi. "There must have been something that I could have done to save Ali. There must have been some way that I could have died in his place."

"No, that is *not* what I mean," said Vörös. His voice cut into her skin, and she flinched. "I mean that the past is over, and to sit and talk about what might have happened is useless. Less than useless. A man is dead because of what I did—I must accept that and go on."

"No," said Kicsi. "I don't think I'll ever accept Ali's death. Ali's and all the rest of them. Why am I alive when they are dead? I'm not worthy. I'm not as good as Ali was, or my mother, or—or anyone that died."

Vörös looked out of the window for a long time. Then he said, "You still want to die, don't you?"

Kicsi said nothing.

"I won't let you die, you know," said Vörös. "The sages say that he who saves a life, it is as though he saved the entire world. How can you throw away your life, your world?"

Kicsi turned to look at him. "I can," she said quietly. They said nothing else for the rest of the trip.

The next few days passed very much like that one. Lulled by the train's rhythm, they slept or stared out the window, saying nothing. At night they would find lodgings, or buy food and continue on to the next station. The bombed stretch of track had been repaired, and they passed it without incident.

One day Kicsi turned from the window and saw at the end of the car a ripple of color, silver and black. "Oh," she said, without meaning to, and stood to see where it had gone.

"What is it, Kicsi?" said Vörös.

"I thought I saw—well, I can't see it anymore. I must have imagined it." She sat down.

"What did you think you saw?"

"Some colors—silver, mostly. Like a piece of silk. I saw a wolf in a zoo once, in Budapest, that was that color."

"Just stay there," said Vörös. "Don't move. I'll be back in a minute."

He walked to the end of the car and looked around carefully. After a while he came back.

"Did you see anything?" said Kicsi.

"No," said Vörös. "It worries me. Tell me again what you saw."

"I—I'm not really sure. It could have been a wolf's tail. But I could have imagined it. I think I was almost asleep."

"I don't think you imagined it," Vörös said.

"Do you think it was the rabbi?"

"Yes," said Vörös. "I do." He looked around the car, frowning slightly. Kicsi shrugged. If the rabbi had followed them, there was nothing she could do. She leaned back and went to sleep.

She woke slowly. Someone was saying something over and over, in a tone of great urgency. "Papers," he said. "Can I see your papers please?"

She opened her eyes, stretched. A young man in uniform stood before them. "We are crossing the border now," he said. "Can I see your papers please?"

"Of course," said Vörös, patting the pockets of his coat. Kicsi relaxed. She had seen him work this slight bit of magic before, at the last border.

"Papers," the man said again. "Can I see your papers please?" He smiled. He had no teeth.

Kicsi moved back. The man's smile grew wider. Everything real and solid fell away into the growing darkness of his mouth. The windows of the train turned black and melted toward each other, eating away the light. Over the noise of the train she heard a roaring, crackling sound, like the last fire of the world.

Vörös shouted words into the din. The walls of the train returned for a moment, then flickered out. Someone else was shouting too, but he stood in the darkness and Kicsi could not hear him. Then both voices were drowned in noise. The darkness grew quickly, like a fire spreading through a dry forest.

Vörös shouted again. The train built itself around them again, gray and unreal. Pieces of the world outside the windows broke through the blackness—a tree, a hill, patches of blue sky. Then the other voice spoke, slow and sure. Darkness crept out of the corners of the train, slower this time, but without stopping. A web of cracks ran from shadow to shadow and widened. A rift appeared at their feet.

Kicsi no longer felt frightened. She knew where she was now. This was the real world that lurked beneath the other one like a skull beneath skin, the world of death. She sat still, waiting for the darkness to take her. Beside her, though she could no longer see him, she heard Vörös speaking slowly, with effort.

The cracks began to close. Something about the secret darkness called to her and she stood up. The floor buckled beneath her. She reached for a rail to hold on to, but the darkness took it first and she jerked her hand away. A small crack opened at her feet and she looked down into it. It widened suddenly as though reaching for her. She prepared to jump.

"No!" said Vörös. "It's me you want, not her! I can escape your illusion, but she can't!"

The other voice laughed. "I know. It was only a warning. Here, I take back my illusion."

The train returned. Around them people were reading, sleeping, talking to each other as though nothing had happened. At the end of the car a man was asking two elderly women for their papers. He had white hair and a bushy mustache.

Kicsi watched the old man warily as he came up to them and asked for their papers. Vörös patted his pockets and the pieces of paper formed beneath his hands, papers that identified them as an importer from Czechoslovakia and his daughter. The old man nodded and continued down the car.

After he had gone Kicsi began to tremble. She realized then that she had been waiting for another illusion like the last one, for another chance at death. She could not sit still. Thoughts chased themselves around and around inside her head. She reached for a newspaper that someone had left behind, but it was in a language she did not understand. The hours passed slowly.

Then she heard someone shout the name of her village, and shout it again, as if the crier wanted to make sure that there had been no mistake. She had known the village was near the border, but she had not realized that they would be coming to it soon. A few people around her stood and reached for their suitcases.

It was evening when the train pulled into the station. At first, as they disembarked, Kicsi thought that nothing was different. But as they walked into the center of the town she could see the small changes. The graveyard was overgrown with weeds, the windows in the synagogue and in some of the houses were smashed. Everything looked older, shabbier.

She was not prepared for the people. At every corner she thought she saw someone she knew—István or László or Sholom. But as she came up to them they always turned into someone else, strangers. Everyone she had known was gone. She felt a terrible weariness.

She sat down on a corner bench. Soldiers were everywhere, laughing, talking, stepping out of houses she had once known. A duck walked down the main street; no one had stayed to care for it. She watched it without curiosity. She was beyond surprises.

Vörös, sitting next to her, said softly, "What do you think?"

She said nothing.

"Kicsi?" said Vörös.

"Go away," Kicsi said.

"What?" said Vörös.

"You heard me. I said go away. I don't want to talk to you."

"Why do you say that?"

"You know why. You know everything, don't you? All I want to do is die. That's all. And you won't even let me do that."

"Are you angry because of what happened this afternoon?"

She turned to him suddenly. "Of course I'm angry! It would have been so easy. I could have jumped, and it would have been all over. It would have been so peaceful then."

"I couldn't let you die."

"'I couldn't let you die,'" she said, mimicking him. "Tell me, do you ever say anything else? And I suppose you expect me to be grateful. You expect me to thank you."

"I don't," said Vörös, but she did not hear him.

"You know," she said, "when I was younger I idolized

127

you. You know that, of course. Now I can't understand why. You don't mean anything to me anymore. When I woke up, in the camp, I didn't even remember who you were."

"That isn't true," said Vörös quietly.

"What do you mean, it isn't true? I didn't recognize you. I remember that."

"You didn't recognize me the second time you saw me," said Vörös. "But you knew quite well who I was the first time."

"The—the first time?"

"When you were lying by the road. After they had given up hope. You looked at me and told me who I was."

"I did?" She frowned. "Something—I remember something now. I was feverish, and I said something silly. I said—wait—" She thought a minute. "I didn't recognize you at all. I said you were a stranger."

"That's right," said Vörös. He paused, as if he waited for something from her.

And then she knew. He was the stranger, the exile, the one who traveled without a home. She had not known what she asked when she had asked long ago to be taken with him. She had not known how much he had envied her and her family as they sat to dinner, or went to the synagogue, or did a hundred ordinary daily tasks. The recent pain she carried with her—the pain of living without a home, without a family—he had carried for a long time, maybe for all of his life. She felt herself opening to him like a flower—the beginning of spring after a long winter. But she could say only, "I spoke your name there, by the side of the road. Your Hebrew name is Gershon—the stranger."

Vörös nodded.

Close—very close—a wolf howled.

Chapter

9

"Quickly," said Vörös. "Run!" He grasped Kicsi by her hand.

"What? Where are we going?" She stood. The wolf howled again.

"Come on!" Vörös said urgently. "Don't you understand? He knows my name. I am as good as dead. We must get to your house and to my pack."

"Oh," said Kicsi. Somehow—she did not remember how —they had started walking, and then running. The roads seemed longer, and darker, and turned in unexpected places. She stumbled against an unlit lamp post and sat down.

"Get up," said Vörös. "Please. We have to go on."

"No," said Kicsi. "You go. I—I'm not well yet. I'm not used to running." She rubbed her sore foot. "Go on without me. I'll only be in the way."

"No," said Vörös. "I need you."

"Need me? For what? Are you still trying to watch me, to make sure that I don't kill myself?"

"No. I need you for something. I don't know what, but I think that it would be good to have you by my side."

"All right." Kicsi stood up slowly. "Let's go."

They walked on. They could barely see in front of them. Houses and trees seemed to move, to block their way. The road twisted like a river.

"I don't like it," said Vörös, moving his hands along a fence. "He is playing with us. The whole village is under his spell."

"I'm so tired," said Kicsi. "Can't I rest for just a little bit?" She leaned against the fence. It seemed to twist itself under her. "Look," she said, pointing to the sky. "He's put out the stars."

"Please," said Vörös. "We have to go on." They started off again. The village curled itself around them like a cat. Every step seemed to take minutes, hours, years. The street flowed away from them, and they could not catch up.

"How much farther is it?" said Kicsi.

"I don't know," said Vörös. "I don't know where we are."

"I feel like I've been walking around in circles."

"We may have been," said Vörös. "I don't know."

Tiny pinpoints of light gathered by the side of the road. "Wolves' eyes," said Kicsi. She shivered.

"Don't stop," said Vörös. "Don't look at them."

"They're . . . terrible," said Kicsi slowly. She wanted desperately to stop, to sit down. The eyes, bright and cold, watched her pitilessly.

"Look!" said Vörös suddenly. "There's Erzsébet's house."

"No," said Kicsi wearily. "It's another illusion. Her house had a tree in front of it. And the curtains were a different color. And the door wasn't brown, it was—" She saw the tree stump under one of the front windows and stopped. "Are we— I guess this is— Well, if this is Erzsébet's house, then our house—my house—must be very close. We're almost there."

They started to run. The points of light that were wolves' eyes fell away from the roadside like falling stars and followed them. Kicsi saw something that looked like a skeleton caught above them in a tree, but Vörös grabbed her and pulled her forward. "Don't stop!" he said, panting, and she ran on behind him. Her side burned with each step.

The wolves drew closer. She felt a sharp pain in her ankle and then a trickle of something moist and warm. Her shoe grew slippery with the blood.

"Almost—there!" said Vörös. "I see it—up ahead."

And then, with no sense of how they had gotten there, they were in front of the house. The wolves fell back. "He is playing with us," Vörös said again, grimly.

"What can we do?" said Kicsi. She stopped, felt the bite on her ankle carefully.

"Do? Nothing. We have to go on."

Together they looked at the house. A sign with Russian letters stood outside the door, but otherwise nothing had changed. A man in uniform sat on the front doorstep, leaning casually on his rifle.

"I don't know if we can get past him," Vörös whispered, but Kicsi was saying, "Come. I know another way. This way."

Kicsi led him around to the side of the house and unlatched the gate carefully. She held it open for him, then followed him into the backyard. No one challenged them. "What is it?" Kicsi whispered. "Why are they here?"

"Quiet," said Vörös. Then, very softly, he said, "It is because of the printing presses. They have taken your house over as their headquarters."

"Oh," she said. They walked quietly across the backyard, past the woodshed, and up to the back door. Vörös tried the door. It was unlocked. "At last," he said. She could almost see him smiling, there in the dark. "A piece of luck for us." He slid the door open and they went inside.

Once inside it was difficult to tell which were the changes made by the soldiers and which created by the rabbi. Corridors sloped away from them and seemed to end at different rooms than they had before. Furniture had been moved around or broken and new furniture brought in. Everything looked much smaller.

"This way," Kicsi whispered. She felt, suddenly, that she did not need to guide them, that the pack itself was calling to them from behind the bricks where she had hidden it so many years ago.

"Go on," Vörös said.

The dimly lit hallway stretched impossibly long before her, and she took a step forward. Suddenly she remembered a dream she had had a long time ago, a dream where she had come home from school and started to greet her mother and father only to find that she was in the wrong house, that she was about to walk up to strangers who had turned from their evening meal and were looking at her with curiosity. She could not go on. This was not her house. She could not intrude here.

"Go on, Kicsi," Vörös said, reassuring her. Very strongly now, she felt the pack ahead of her. She touched the wall with one hand and began to walk.

As her eyes got used to the darkness, as she followed the cunning twistings and turnings of the corridor, she began to hear the noises of the house. Ahead of her, in the living room, men were singing and laughing. She could hear the thump of a dice cup and the hoarse voices of the soldiers rising after each turn, and she felt a sudden unreasoning anger that these men were using the table her mother had cleaned and polished so often. Then she remembered where she was, and the anger passed.

Somone was humming tunelessly in the kitchen. She followed the sound. The walls shifted suddenly. "Here," she said, stopping in front of the hall outside the pantry. "This is where I hid it." The feeling that they were near the pack was very strong now.

Vörös knelt and began to pry out the bricks. "Pavel!" someone called from the living room. The steady rhythmic thump of the dice cup had stopped. "Pavel, we need some more sugar for the tea. More sugar, please!"

"Of course!" the man in the kitchen called. Then softer, to himself, he said, "More sugar." Kicsi and Vörös could hear him stand up, could hear him as he came out to the pantry. The walls flowed around them and closed in. They had no place to run.

They stood. In the distance they could hear Pavel begin to hum again, and then stop. He turned a corner and stood before them, a squat young man with a few days' growth of beard. "What are you doing here?" he said.

Vörös walked over to him and pushed him lightly in the chest. He fell against the brick wall and slid to the floor. "What are you doing here?" he repeated, but Kicsi could see that his eyes had closed. "What are you doing here?"

"Can't you—make him stop?" Kicsi asked.

"No," said Vörös. "I can't." He returned to the wall and pried out one brick, then another. A space wide enough for Kicsi's hand opened up. From the living room someone called again, "Pavel!"

"Hurry!" Vörös said.

Kicsi felt behind the brick wall for the pack. For a minute she could not find it and panic took hold of her. Then she touched it, lifted it out, held it in her hands. As she looked at it, she felt for the first time that she had come home.

"What are you doing here?" Pavel said again.

"Here," Kicsi said softly. She passed the pack to Vörös. "Let's go, quickly."

Someone from the living room called, "Pavel!" and swore. "All right, then," the man in the living room said. "I'll come get it myself!" Vörös heard him start toward the kitchen. They turned and ran back the way they had come.

Kicsi felt time, place, memory fold over and become confused. She was not in her house at all now, but in Erzsébet's; she was in her house again, but Aladár was watching her put away the pack and saying, "Maybe everything you've told me is true." Corridors beckoned, each one a different path toward a different future. She could not find Vörös. Without the pack to guide her she was lost within the maze of her own house.

She chose one corridor and began to walk. There was her bed with the goose feather quilt neatly tucked into the sides—but what was it doing in the hallway? There was the lamp she had loved as a child, with a beautiful woman's head at its base, but the shade was gone, and one of the bulbs was out. And whose couch was that? Erzsébet's family had had a couch like it once, but it had been red, not green . . . Things floated toward her and drifted away. She felt, stronger this time, that she was dreaming. There was nothing to hold on to. She clenched her fists.

"Vörös," she whispered. She gathered courage from the sound of her voice and said, louder, "Vörös!" There was no answer.

She tripped against something and looked down. She had stumbled against one of the bricks that Vörös had taken out of the wall. Had she truly gone anywhere at all? Or had she stayed in the pantry and imagined it all? Near her Pavel sat propped against the wall. His lips moved, but he made no sound.

"Pavel!" someone called from the kitchen, the same man who had called to Pavel before. It had taken him an eternity to go from the living room to the kitchen. "What happened to you? Where are you?"

His footsteps sounded nearer. The thump of the dice cup came louder, like heartbeats. Desperately Kicsi opened the door to the kitchen and looked inside. She saw smoke and ashes, and the outline of barbed wire. The sound of the dice cups became the clatter of machine guns.

She gasped and closed the door quickly. "Pavel!" the man called. "I can't see you. Something's happened to the lights . . ."

She turned. Something moved at the edge of her vision, and she turned again. The fat gray cat, the cat that Sarah had stayed to feed, came toward her.

The cat could not possibly still be alive. Yet it continued to walk toward her, brushing against her legs. She could not feel it against her. It walked down the hall to a point where three corridors converged and without hesitation chose the left one.

Kicsi followed it. She came up behind it and called to it, but it ran lightly away from her. It turned a corner, and Kicsi recognized with a start the back hallway. The cat walked up to the back door and was gone. Kicsi did not see it go. She opened the back door and stepped outside.

The night was as dark as the inside of caves. She breathed in the cold air. "Vörös," she whispered. "Vörös, where are you?" For the first time she felt real fear, as she wondered what would happen to her if the rabbi found her without Vörös.

"Over here," someone whispered, and, very dimly, she could see the outline of a black coat. "Step over this way. The gate's over here."

Carefully, Vörös in front, they went across the yard toward the gate. Vörös unlatched the gate and stepped through. Kicsi followed a few paces behind him. Suddenly Kicsi heard Vörös stop and gasp aloud. Before them, where there had been only empty road, stood the rabbi.

He was thinner than Kicsi remembered, and taller. His gray-black hair streamed out behind him. A light shone in his eyes, a light that was not a reflection of the stars, which had been put out, or of the lamps, which had not been lit. Kicsi crouched near the gatepost.

He lifted his hand. The pack flew out of Vörös's hand and landed without a sound a few feet away, near Kicsi. Vörös took a step back.

"You are a dead man, traveler," said the rabbi.

"Yes," said Vörös.

"You are a dead man," the rabbi went on, as though he had not heard Vörös speak, "for three reasons. I know your name. You no longer have your pack. And here, where I have lived all my life, my magic is stronger than yours. My magic comes from the people and the strength of my village. That is a strength you do not know."

"Yes."

"So." The rabbi stepped back slightly. Kicsi could see them both clearly then—two figures dressed in black, facing each other without speaking. Why doesn't he do something? Kicsi thought.

The rabbi began to speak. Mist washed around him, began to take on form. Kicsi heard the rabbi speak Vörös's name, his true name—Gershon, the stranger. She thought she could see in the mist old women and young boys, men in fancy furs and hats and men wearing farmer's clothing. She saw people dressed in ancient armor, carrying swords, and skeletons with jewels winking on the bones of their fingers. A shape with no head held the hand of a small boy wearing tatters. A muffled sound, of sword against iron, of sighing, came from the figures.

She knew them, the dead from the synagogue. She should have warned Vörös. She remembered a day long ago, standing in front of the synagogue with Aladár . . .

"These are the unavenged dead," said the rabbi. "They have been killed in wars or in pogroms. Some have been killed so long ago that only they remember the name of their oppressor. They came to the town foretelling catastrophe and I bound them to me. They will do as I say now. If I tell them to avenge themselves on you, they will."

Vörös nodded. "Then they are very much like you, rabbi," he said. "You want your revenge, and because there is no one else, you will avenge yourself on me."

"No," said the rabbi. "Because you killed my daughter."

"I did not kill your daughter, rabbi."

"You did. Just as surely as if you sent her to the furnaces yourself. Why did you speak the words of evil omen at her wedding if you did not want her dead?"

"I was—I was not myself. I saw the deaths coming, and I wanted your people to be warned."

The rabbi said nothing. He leaned against his cane and looked down at the road for a moment. Vörös turned and took a step back, toward his pack. Fire leapt from the ground, singeing his coat. "You lie!" said the rabbi, looking up at Vörös from under his bushy eyebrows. "I will listen to your tales no longer."

The dead stirred at the sound of fire. Behind her, Kicsi felt, without seeing it, Vörös's pack.

"All right, then," said Vörös. "Perhaps there is someone else I can reason with. You, over there. From your looks I would say you lived and died over a hundred years ago. What is your quarrel with me?"

The man in the mists that Vörös pointed to said nothing.

"Do I look like the man who killed you?" Vörös asked. "What is your business here?"

"Fire killed me, traveler," said the man. His voice was thin and whispering, like a broken teakettle. "They came in the night, on horseback, setting fire to our houses, stealing our cattle. I was powerless against them. All my life I have felt powerless, and never so much so as at the moment of my death. And when I kill you, I will feel power for the first time. After that, I can sleep peacefully."

The rabbi fell back into the mist of the dead. "I have followed you across Europe to kill you," said the rabbi. "We waste time, talking like this."

Fire flew out toward Vörös from among the dead. He caught it in his hand and sent it back, and it disappeared into the ranks of the dead. Another flame, from another place, came toward Vörös, and again he sent it back.

"Where is he?" Kicsi heard him say. "If I could see him, I might— He is playing with me." Again Vörös tried to step back, and again he was whipped by fire.

"You're mad," he said. "All of you, you're all mad. I did not kill her!"

"Do you think that that matters, traveler?" said another of the dead. Water streamed from her hair and clothes. "We want blood. We have waited long enough."

Vörös took a deep breath. He stood very still and began to speak. The mist lessened, and the rabbi seemed to stand forward, a blurred black outline. Vörös let his breath out slowly, gathering strength. He raised his hand.

The mist enfolded the rabbi, wrapping him around like a cloak. Laughter rose from the dead, a dry muffled sound like stones rubbing together. Vörös dropped his arms.

The dead moved again. Kicsi watched as the mist turned

to shapes of people, each one crying for revenge. She saw a tall man on horseback, an archer, a woman holding a candle. Something behind her called to her, called strongly, but she could not move her eyes.

The man on horseback sent a flame out toward Vörös. Vörös caught it quickly and sent it back, and it disappeared into the mist. His face twisted with pain. He was panting, and sweat ran into his eyes.

"Stand back!" Vörös called, and the power in his voice was such that the dead waited, restless. "What will you do after you kill me, rabbi?"

The rabbi looked at the road again. It seemed to Kicsi that he was confused for a moment, that he was considering the strange events that had led him back to his village to kill a man. He was very tired.

Finally he looked up. "That does not matter," he said. "What comes afterward is none of your concern."

The dead moved forward again, covering the road, crying aloud in fierce voices. Kicsi could hear them only faintly, as though they were calling to her from beneath the water.

They were very close to Vörös now. When they kill him, she thought, will they come for me? She felt, much stronger than before, that she should turn around, that there was something very important that she had forgotten to do. She looked over her shoulder and saw Vörös's pack.

Then time seemed to stop for her, to remain poised between one stroke of the pendulum and the next. Two voices argued within her head like Rachel and the gray-haired woman arguing over her life long ago.

Save him, one said.

Why should I?

Why? You care about him.

No, I don't. I don't care about anyone but myself, and I want to die. That's all I care about.

You cared about Ali, once.

Y—yes, I did. What about it?

Ali would want you to save him.

Ali is dead.

Ah, and you want to join him. You think you can be as heroic as he was, simply by dying. But it doesn't take courage to die. That's easy. It takes courage to live. Ali had that courage.

Ali would—would want me to live?

Ali would, and so would your parents. Your family. Do you honestly think they would want to see you die?

M—maybe not. But I want to. I want to die.

That isn't true. You don't want to die, not really.

I—I don't?

No. Why did you run?

I ran because—because Vörös forced me. Because I had no choice.

Certainly you had a choice. You didn't have to stay with Vörös. There was nothing he could have done to keep you with him. You want to live. You want to, but you don't think you have the right.

That's right. What have I done? I don't deserve—

Done? You have done nothing yet. But no one deserves their life. It is a gift, given to all. It is not for you to decide whether or not you deserve it. But if you want a chance to prove yourself, that too is given to you now. You can save the life of someone you love, so that he does not die like Aladár. There has been too much death. He who saves a life, it is as though he saved the entire world.

Then time started again, the pendulum began its downward stroke. Without thinking, Kicsi knew what she had to do. She opened the pack and felt along the necklaces and amulets and herbs until she found a small leather bag tied with a ribbon.

She held the bag in her hand, then lifted it and threw it toward Vörös. Pain lay open her head, her stomach. A darkness that was not the night came and claimed her. She fell to the street.

She wondered, when she opened her eyes, who had won. Vörös, probably, since the dead had not come for her. But the rabbi and Vörös still stood and faced each other. Her eyes had closed for only a few seconds.

The dead moved forward, rippling like clouds across water. And Vörös still stood against them, black, not moving. Then she saw that he held something in his hands. A leather bag.

Vörös opened the bag and poured its contents into his hand. There was a ruby red as the core of fire, a sapphire blue as the depths of the sea, a diamond white as the stars fused together. He threw the ruby into the air, and it expanded, became a red juggling ball. The other stones followed it. Soon he was balancing seven balls in the air.

Kicsi almost laughed. Of all the things he could have done, this was certainly the least expected. And yet he looked so fine standing there, his face changing colors as different colors shone upon it, that she knew he had done the right thing, the thing he had come to the village to do. Many years later, when she would think of him, she would remember him standing like that, a strange mixture of the familiar and the unexpected. She felt a great love for him. She knew then that she was going to live.

The mist had stopped. The light of the balls fell on the faces of the dead, turning them blue, red, green. Their mouths were open, and they called for revenge in languages living and dead.

"You have said, rabbi," Vörös said, "that you know my name. That is true, but it is also true I know yours. You have said that I do not have my pack. That is no longer true, as you can see. And you have said that your magic is stronger than mine because we are in your village, and your magic comes from the strength of your people, the people of the village. But, rabbi, where are your people? The village you knew is gone, rabbi. You have no magic left."

The rabbi remained hidden among the dead. Vörös let his hands fall to his side. The balls continued to circle, but slower now, moving with the heavy grace of planets circling the sun. Kicsi could see Vörös's face as it became orange, blue, red.

"Do you hear me, rabbi? You cannot kill me. The source of your magic is gone. Look."

A picture appeared within the circle of the balls—a picture of the town as Kicsi and Vörös had seen it earlier that day. Houses were deserted, left open. Strangers walked in the streets. Vörös showed them the synagogue, another deserted house. Its paint was peeling, and many of the windows were gone. Dirt piled up in the courtyard.

The picture changed as they looked at it. They could see the inside of the synagogue now. Rows of chairs had been ripped out, as well as the ornamental fence dividing the men and the women. The ark was open and the Torah was gone. Wind blew in through the open windows.

"Where is your congregation, rabbi?" said Vörös. "Where are your people?"

The mists flowed back. "Dead," said the rabbi softly.

"Where is your village now, rabbi? Where is the center of your life?"

"Gone," said the rabbi. "I am powerless."

Kicsi felt the mist begin to move, to re-form itself. She knew what had happened then. The rabbi had listened to Vörös and had believed him. He had lost control over the dead. And the dead, sensing his nearness, had come after him for their revenge.

Kicsi was able to see the rabbi now, leaning on his cane, standing in the middle of an empty circle. The dead had turned on him, and they were closing in.

Vörös reached out suddenly with his hand. His fingers closed over something, and when they opened again Kicsi could see the red ball caught within his palm. The other balls in the circle closed in to fill the gap.

He strode into the mists. Light from the ball fell upon the dead, turning them the color of blood, giving them the look of life, of health. One of the dead laughed, a high, awful sound, and the illusion of life was broken.

"Here," Vörös said to the rabbi, giving him the red ball. "Take this. Quickly." The rabbi took it gratefully, saying nothing. The light dimmed for a moment, then shone out again.

Vörös turned to the dead. "You," he said. "Stand back. You will stand back."

The terrible laughter came again. Vörös turned quickly toward the sound. A young woman with an upraised sword came toward him. She had a gaping wound in her side. "Stand back," said Vörös. "Do you think your ghostly sword can touch me? Stand back. You shall not harm him or me."

The woman came forward. Her sword cut through the air in front of her, and the dead moved from her path.

"I know you," said Vörös with amazement. "I fought with you against the same oppressor, many, many years ago. I understand your pain. I feel your death blow. I can help you sleep again. Listen to me, Shoshana."

Vörös began to sing, a slow, soothing melody. The woman dropped the point of her sword. She sank toward the ground.

From another part of the mist the archer moved suddenly, stringing his bow. "Vörös!" the rabbi called. "Look out!"

Vörös said three sharp words and the string of the bow snapped, wrapping around the archer's fingers. He cried out in pain and fell back.

More of the dead were moving now, coming toward Vörös in groups of three and four. "I cannot hold them all," said Vörös. "I need your help."

"My help?" said the rabbi. "I have no help to give. My powers are gone. You told me that."

"Don't be a fool," said Vörös. "You should not believe what a man says when he is fighting for his life."

The rabbi laughed. "I can give you their names, at least," he said. "Perhaps we can hold them together."

"We can," said Vörös. "We will have to."

The dead surrounded them. Kicsi could see a shape wearing a golden crown and a long cloak full of holes. The woman with no head was there, as was the skeleton with the jewels on his fingers. They fell upon Vörös and the rabbi like waves upon tall rocks and retreated, fell and retreated, as one by one Vörös or the rabbi sent them back to their uneasy sleep. Sometimes Kicsi could see only a white swirling mist, with red light staining the center like blood. Sometimes she could see the two magicians standing clear of the mist, resting for a moment until the dead closed over them again.

The woman whose hair and clothes streamed with water came toward them. Her face and hands were blue, and her eyes glistened like marble. "I was a small sorceress in my way," she said. "I dealt mostly in death by drowning. I can still remember a few tricks. First I will put out that fire you have there."

Water drenched the rabbi's hand. The light of the red ball flickered and died.

"We have no water here," the woman said, "which is unfortunate. But I can make you believe that you are drowning, that water is filling your lungs, that you cannot breathe . . ." She spoke on and on. Her voice was a trickle of water, a brook, a river, an ocean.

The two men stood gaping at her. Their eyes opened and closed, and their hands clutched at the air around them. Vörös felt his way toward the rabbi, slowly, as though moving against a strong tide.

"Soon you will cease to struggle," the woman said, "and the tide will take you. You will have no worries then. It is very pleasant to surrender yourself to the water. I know. I did it myself."

The rabbi stood without moving. Vörös reached out and took the red ball from his hand, and the light blazed forth once again. Vörös opened his eyes and looked at the woman.

"Return to the lake in which you were drowned, sorceress," he said. "We will not listen to you here."

The woman seemed to grow taller. Her hair shone like a waterfall. Then she swayed slowly, rippling like a river, and was gone.

The mist thinned to a network of roots, to small webs, to nothing. Vörös and the rabbi were left standing alone on the gravel roads of the village, saying nothing, facing each other. It was almost morning.

"I—I do not know what to say, traveler," the rabbi said. "You saved my life."

Vörös said nothing.

"I was wrong, then," said the rabbi. The wild light was gone from his eyes. "You did not want to kill me."

"No."

"And you did not kill my daughter."

"No," said Vörös. "I did not."

"I misunderstood you," the rabbi said. "For a magician, that is a very dangerous thing to do."

"It is over now," said Vörös. He held the red ball awkwardly. "We can forget it. It does not matter."

"No," said the rabbi. "It matters. I know now that you did not kill my daughter. And I know who did kill her. I—I have always known. It is a knowledge from which I have been trying to hide since she died, but I can run from it no longer. I am trapped here at the end of my road. You did not kill her, traveler. I did."

"You!" said Vörös, but the rabbi raised a hand.

"Let me speak," he said. "Did you think that you were the only one who could see the future? I too saw the flames and the furnaces, and I knew that I was given this sight to warn my people, to prepare them for the dangers to come. But I did not believe." The rabbi sighed, leaning forward against his cane. He looked like a weary old man now, nothing more. "You, traveler, you have been around the world and have seen what people can do to each other. I have only been in one small village. I did not believe that such cruelty could exist. I ignored the warning."

He paused, took a deep breath. "Then you came, stirring up the people, sounding the warnings. I hated you then. I believed that if we could only forget about the horrors they would not come to pass. In many ways, as you know, I am a stubborn old man. I sent you from the village.

"But the horrors came anyway. I was in a neighboring town, visiting a colleague of mine. I had gone for a walk, and when I returned I found that they had arrested my wife and were soon to arrest me. I did not know what to do, what to think. I changed into a wolf.

"I spent a year in beast's form, existing like a beast. I lived from one day to the next, from one meal to the next, not worrying about the world, the future. I knew that my wife and daughter were dead, but I could have saved others, as—as you did, traveler. But I did not. I could not face the world or my cowardice.

"And then I found you. I blamed you for everything then, because I could not blame myself. I was crazy—crazy with unhappiness—" He bent his head, his shoulders shaking with his grief. "You did not kill her, traveler," the rabbi said. "I did. I could have done something. . . ."

"No," said Kicsi. She stood up from where she had hidden and came forward.

Vörös turned to her. "Kicsi!" he said. "Stay back. Please." Ha, she thought, almost pleased. I have never surprised him with anything before.

"No," she said. "I—I have something to say. You are wrong, rabbi. You did not kill your daughter. And it does not matter now if you could have done something to save her or not. To talk about what might have happened is useless. You can think about what might have happened, turn it over and over in your mind until you can't think of anything else. You can plan your revenge or—or suicide. But none of that can change the past. The dead—your daughter and my parents—they would want us to go on. To live." She was crying now. She wiped away the tears angrily. "Do you understand?"

"No," the rabbi said. "I cannot understand. I am an old man, and a stubborn one. It does not seem right to me, as it does to you, that so many people should die and that we should say only, 'Ah, well, but that is the past. There is nothing we can do about it now.' It is a terrible thing, a thing beyond my understanding. All my life I have lived with things I can understand—my family, my village, my traditions. And now, at the end of my life, I am faced with something I cannot accept or understand. I don't—I don't know what to do. There is nothing that I can do."

"No, I don't mean that," Kicsi said, nervously. She had never spoken back to the rabbi before, and she was not sure of what she would say to him. "I don't mean that we should forget or—or do nothing. I mean that—well— You knew my parents, rabbi."

The rabbi nodded.

"And Aladár, Erzsi's cousin?"

"Yes, slightly."

"They are dead now. And I—I wanted to die too, because —I don't know if I can explain this to you—because I knew that I wasn't as good as they were. It didn't seem fair that they should die and I should live."

"But that—that's nonsense," the rabbi said. "Of course you should live."

"I know. I know that now," said Kicsi. "But don't you see? You're doing exactly what I did. You blame yourself for something that was not your doing."

The rabbi looked at Vörös. "She is very wise," he said. "Have you been teaching her?"

Vörös smiled. "No," he said. "She has come to her wisdom by herself. I am very proud of her."

"It will be hard," the rabbi said, not looking at Vörös or Kicsi, "to give up my vengeance. It has occupied my mind for so long. I will have to start thinking about the world again, and about my dead. I see now that I must give it up, this foolish idea I once had. But what will I do now? Where will I go?"

"Why don't you stay here?" Vörös said. "People will be coming back someday. There will be a community here again, though not as big as it was before. They will need a rabbi, someone to lead them, to help them get settled again."

"No," said the rabbi. "I can never lead anyone again. I do not understand the world, and I can't pretend to the villagers that I do. They will be asking me questions for which I do not have the answers.

"I think," the rabbi said slowly, "that I would like to find the answers. That I would like to travel the world, and to learn. To become a student again, as I was when I was younger. Why did my daughter have to die? I understand now that you are not to blame, traveler, and it may be true, as this young woman has said, that I am not to blame. But I would like to think that there was a—a reason for her death, and for the deaths of so many other people. It may be that there is no answer. It may be—it is likely—that I shall die before I find it. But I cannot accept that her death, so young, had no meaning. That is something I cannot understand."

Vörös nodded. There was pity in his eyes. "I wish you luck, rabbi," he said.

"Thank you," said the rabbi. *"Sholom aleichem.* And good-bye, Kicsi. I will always remember your words." He walked away, his feet making no sound on the gravel-paved road, and merged with the shadows. They were never to see him again.

Kicsi felt suddenly tired. She yawned and leaned against the gatepost. Just before she closed her eyes she looked up and saw the juggling balls circling over her head, crowning her with precious jewels. Then she fell asleep, and did not wake even when Vörös lifted her in his arms and carried her away.

Chapter

10

Invisible, she walked through the rooms and corridors of the house. Outside it was bright afternoon, and things were clearer than they had been last night. She saw that much of what she had seen the night before was real and not part of the rabbi's illusion. Furniture had been moved around or exchanged to make room for all the soldiers staying in the house. She reached out to touch a vase and her fingers went through it. Vörös had told her that that would happen.

That morning she had talked to Vörös, telling him that she wanted to see her house for the last time. "I can make you invisible," he had said.

"No, I meant—Maybe I could get through the back door again."

"I wouldn't try it. Not during the day."

"You could . . . make me invisible?"

"Of course," Vörös had said, smiling. "Don't make any noise, though. They'll still be able to hear you. And you won't be able to touch anything. If you wanted to, you could walk right through the walls."

Now she looked at the solid walls around her and decided she did not want to try it. If she walked through them she would feel even more like a ghost come back to haunt the scenes of its former life. She went down the back hall and into the kitchen.

"Don't tell me you didn't see it," one of the soldiers was saying. "All kinds of bright lights and strange shapes, right outside the front window. I thought for a moment we were under attack again, but there wasn't any sound. Strangest thing I ever saw."

The other soldiers laughed. "I swear to you, I didn't see a thing," one said. "I must have slept right through it."

"And Pavel had some kind of fit last night," the first soldier said. "I don't really know about this place. I've been talking to one of the villagers, and he says there used to be a rabbi here who could—well, they called him some sort of magician. And the woods are supposed to be haunted. All right, laugh! Still, I'll be glad when we're posted somewhere else."

Kicsi smiled at that. The fat gray cat came into the kitchen, and one of the soldiers fed it scraps from the sink. It jumped into his lap and began to purr loudly. So the cat had survived too, Kicsi thought. She felt a kind of sadness that it had found another life apart from her family.

She went on into the dining room. The huge dining table was set out as though for company. She remembered the last night that they were all together, the Passover night more than a year ago, and she began to cry, softly, so the soldiers would not hear. It was the first time she had cried properly for her dead.

She did not want to see any more. Vörös had told her that the spell would end when she stepped out the front door. She stumbled through the living room, walked through the door, and left the house for the last time.

Vörös waited for her in the woods. She said nothing to him, but nodded and walked past him toward the forest's center. He smiled at her as she went.

Toward evening she came back. Vörös had built a small fire. "Are you ready to go?" he asked.

"Go?" she said. "I don't know where I could go to."

"Your brother and sister are waiting for you," Vörös said. "At the Displaced Persons camp in Italy."

"I suppose," she said. "I know I have to leave. There's nothing for me here. I know that now. But I don't know if

I can face them, so soon . . ." She did not finish her thought.

"That's no problem," Vörös said. "We'll leave tomorrow, if you like, and we'll take our time getting to the camp. The journey will be good for you."

Kicsi nodded. The doubt was gone from her face. "All right," she said.

"How do you feel?" Vörös asked.

"Better," Kicsi said. She laughed. "I feel as if I could start on a long trip tomorrow. I certainly didn't feel like that yesterday."

"Yes," said Vörös. "You've changed quite a bit."

Kicsi laughed again. "Did I surprise you?"

Vörös did not answer, but sat and looked into the fire for a time. Then: "Yes, you did," he said.

She caught the deeper meaning of his words and shivered. "You mean—you did not think that I would survive the night." It was not a question.

"No," he said. "I did not. And if you had died, it would have meant more to me, almost, than the deaths of all those people I could not save during the war. I love you very much, Kicsi."

They sat together for a while, not speaking, watching the fire hiss and spark. "Why did you throw me my leather bag, Kicsi?" Vörös said at last.

"Why?" Kicsi said. "Because I wanted to save you, of course. Because I didn't want to see you die."

"I don't think that's what I meant," Vörös said. "I don't know if I can explain it. How did you know that of all the things in my sack I would be needing the leather bag?"

Kicsi blinked. "I don't know," she said. "I just knew you would. Why? Is it important?"

"I don't know," Vörös said. "It means that you have been touched by magic—that magic has left a mark on you as permanent as that scar on your palm. All your life you will know things without knowing how you knew them. I don't think that's such a terrible thing. After all," he said laughing, "it saved my life."

"I'm glad," Kicsi said. "I'm glad that I could do it. I don't care so much about the magic. It doesn't seem as important to me now as it did once."

"Well," Vörös said. "Tomorrow will be a long day for

us. Why don't we have something to eat and then go to sleep early?"

Light was just striking the road as they stepped out of the forest the next morning. Vörös carried his pack over his shoulder. As they came into the town, Kicsi saw a chimney sweep. She flinched. Then, with a great effort, she pointed him out to Vörös.

Vörös had been watching her carefully. He relaxed when he saw her point at the chimney sweep. "Do you want to make a wish?" he said lightly.

"I've had enough of wishes," she said. "And I'll be seeing more of faraway places than I ever wanted to. I wonder—what will America be like? Is it like here?"

"Parts of it are," Vörös said. "Of course, parts of it are very different." He led her a roundabout route, so that they did not pass her house, or the graveyard, or the synagogue, and he talked all the while, telling her stories of faraway places. She understood what he was doing, and she was grateful for it. She did not want to talk until they had left the village. They came to the railroad station and boarded the train without looking back.

The trip going away from the village, she thought, should have been the same as the trip coming in, but it was not. Of the trip coming in she remembered only darkness—the night they had spent in the forest, the black cracks in the railroad car. As they journeyed out she was surprised to see that it was summer. The sun shone hot on the rails of the train, and they seemed to stretch out forever, like a summons, or a promise. The train windows showed wheat fields under the heat or trees heavy with summer leaves. Kicsi watched it all, fascinated.

Sometimes she would turn to Vörös and ask him for stories. He told her a little of what he had done during the war, and she told him about the time she thought she had seen him in the camp. He told her of his wanderings after the war, and how he had come finally to the camp to find her lying by the roadside. She asked him to tell her that story again and again, and as he told it she would not look at him but at the scar on her palm. Now that she wanted to live again she was amazed that her life had hung on such a small thing as that scar. "Touched by magic," she said, and Vörös agreed.

At dusk they passed the inn where they had been asked to leave and the forest in which they had spent the night. They pointed out the town to each other, and then both quickly changed the subject.

They slept that night on the train. Sometime during the night Kicsi jerked awake, and Vörös woke after her. She fell back asleep, and when she woke the next morning she said nothing about her night, but sat and stared out the train window. They had come out of the small town. Forests sloped away from them on either side.

That afternoon she asked suddenly, "Can you do anything about dreams?"

"What do you mean?" Vörös said.

"I mean if a person's having a dream he doesn't want to have, and he has the same dream over and over, can you do anything about it? Can you stop it?"

"What dreams are you having, Kicsi?" Vörös said.

Kicsi said nothing for a moment. Then she said softly, "I dream my family's still alive. My family and Aladár. I dream that they got away somehow, and that we all meet together somewhere. In America, I guess. And we're all very happy, and then someone says to them, 'But you can't be here. You died in the war.' And they disappear, and I wake up."

"What's wrong with the dream, Kicsi? It shows you loved your family very much."

"Yes, I did. You're right. But I'm so happy in the dream, and then I wake up, and I remember . . . Every night. I think it's real, every night."

"You'll always have the pain, Kicsi. It will get less as the years pass, and the dreams will stop eventually. And you have people you can share your grief with—Tibor and Ilona. That will be important. But I can't do anything about the pain. You don't know how often I've wished I could."

"That's what I thought," Kicsi said. "But I had to ask."

One day she noticed that the trees outside her window were different. The days were warmer. They were journeying south, to a part of Europe she had never seen. Until then she had traveled almost complacently, not really worrying about the future. Now panic overwhelmed her.

Once again she would be facing something outside her experience.

"Why can't you come with me to America?" she asked Vörös.

"I can't. There are people who need me here."

"Vörös." She looked at him, seeing something she had never seen in him before. "How long have you been traveling like this, helping people? How old are you?"

"Older than I look," he said, smiling. He saw that that was not enough for her and went on. "Older than you or your father or the rabbi. A long time ago I studied magic, traveling for many years with one of the greatest magicians in Europe. It was he who taught me the power of names and who gave me the healing spell that kept me young past the time allowed to me. I lived among many peoples and learned from them the details of their lives—how to ride a horse, how to shoot with a bow and arrow, how to build a shelter from the wind and rain. I learned to speak their languages. And when I returned home, long after my parents' death, I found the people there strange—unsubtle men who knew nothing of the world outside their small village. When my teacher died I left the town for the last time. And so I have wandered ever since, going where I am needed."

Kicsi sat silent, listening to him. "There are—there are people who need you in America, too," she said finally, not looking at him.

"I know," Vörös said. "But I will not be in America for a long time. I'm sorry, Kicsi."

"You mean—I'll never see you again."

"Yes," said Vörös. "But you're strong enough now that you won't need me anymore."

"I know," Kicsi said. "But—Vörös—I'm going to miss you."

"I'll miss you too," Vörös said. "If you like, I can give you something to remember me by."

She almost agreed. Then she remembered and said. "No. Something will happen to it, and I'll lose it, like I lost the last one." She was very close to tears, but instead of crying she laughed, a quick, high-pitched sound. "And anyway," she said, "I'll never need anything to remember you by."

A few days later they got off in a crowded, busy city.

She could not remember ever seeing so many people in one place, and she held on to Vörös's hand for comfort. Cars honked at them as they ran across the street. Buildings were taller and closer together than she was used to. People rushed past them without looking around. They took a bus to the outskirts of the city.

They got off in front of what used to be an army barracks. Vörös walked into the first building he saw and Kicsi followed him. Inside was a desk piled high with papers, but no one was in the office. They turned to leave. At that moment the telephone began to ring.

After it had rung three times a young man ran into the office, nodded to Vörös and Kicsi, and picked up the phone. "Hello," he said in English. It was then that Kicsi realized with amazement that she was seeing her first American.

She could not follow his conversation, though she remembered enough from school to know that it was about a ship due to leave the next week. "Ten people!" he said at one point. "I'll have to have more than that. Ten people won't even make a dent in the crowd we've got here." Finally he said, "All right. See if you can get me some more spaces. I know . . . I know. Thank you. Bye."

He hung up and looked at Vörös. "I'm sorry," he said. "I just don't know what to do here. They say they can let me send ten of these people to America. Ten! Out of the whole camp. I don't know. . . . Well, anyway. What can I do for you?"

"We want to see some people," Vörös said.

"Fine," said the man. "Go right in."

"But don't you—don't you have records?"

"Records?" The man laughed. "You're kidding, aren't you? There's too many of them. We've tried keeping records of the people that died once, but we didn't know most of their names. Some of these people don't even remember their names themselves. No, if you're looking for people, the best way to do it is to go out and look for yourself."

"All right," Vörös said. "Come on, Kicsi."

They went out into the barracks. "What did he say?" Kicsi said.

"He doesn't know if Tibor or Ilona are here," Vörös said. "We'll have to look for them ourselves."

Kicsi looked around her. Everyone seemed much healthier than Kicsi remembered from the camps. Couples held hands and walked together in the sunshine. She could not see Tibor or Ilona.

They searched for about an hour, then rested on the steps of one of the buildings. "Is that them?" Kicsi heard someone say in Hungarian. She turned to look.

"It looks like them, Sándor," someone else said. "A tall man with red hair and a young woman. That's what they said." Two men came forward hesitantly.

"Are you—do they call you Vörös?" Sándor asked.

"Yes," Vörös said.

"Good," said Sándor. "I have something for you. It's from Tibor and Ilona. They said that they knew you."

"What about them?" said Kicsi. Panic, the same sort of panic she had felt when she realized that Vörös would leave her soon, hit her like a wave. She had learned how quickly death could come, how unstable the world really was. "Are they all right?"

"Yes, they're fine," Sándor said, laughing. "They're better off than we are, anyway. They say—wait. I'd better show you the note they left."

They followed him to his barracks and waited outside while he got the note. "Here it is," Sándor said, coming out of the door. He handed the note to Kicsi. "They said I should give it to you."

She opened it. "Dear Kicsi," it said. "We got a chance to go to America and decided that we couldn't wait. We hope you'll follow us soon. Maybe Vörös can help you. We'll be staying with our cousins in New York. We look forward to seeing you. All our love, Ilona."

"So they've gone to America already," Kicsi said.

"They felt badly about leaving you here," Sándor said, "but it was a chance they couldn't refuse. They thought that you would be able to make it to America on your own. I don't know how," he went on, glumly. "I've heard rumors that there's only space for ten people on the next ship."

"Really?" said Vörös. He was smiling, and his blue eyes were round with amazement. "I've heard there will be space for fifteen." He looked at Kicsi.

"If you say so," Kicsi said. She was smiling too.

"Fifteen!" Sándor said. "That's good news. But—what are you laughing at?"

"I don't know," Kicsi said. "I don't think I could explain it to you, anyway."

Kicsi spent the night at the DP camp. She found a spare bed and took the evening meal with everyone else. No one noticed that she did not belong there. Vörös was gone for most of the night and the next morning.

He returned in time for the noon meal and slipped into the seat beside Kicsi. All around them were the sounds of forks hitting tin trays, of water being poured into tin cups, of conversation as people sat down to eat. "He will make the announcement very soon," Vörös said to her, and at that moment the American walked to the front of the room.

"Attention!" the American said, and an interpreter repeated him in a few languages. "Can I have your attention!" The room quieted. People were turning to face front. "A ship will be leaving for America next week." Everyone nodded. That had been a camp rumor for weeks. "We have space on board for fifteen people—" Talk sprang up—"Not ten!" "I told you, the man I talked to said fifteen." "Fifteen! Maybe we have a chance this time" —until the American called for quiet. "Quiet, please! Please be quiet. I'm going to read the names of the people who will be going."

Kicsi was not surprised that she was included among the fifteen people, though she had hoped until the last name was called that Vörös would be going too. She was surprised when the American called out Sándor's name. "Thank you," she whispered to Vörös. "I would never have thought of him."

"Thank you for what?" Vörös said, but his eyes held the same amusement as yesterday. Kicsi thought she could not remember another time that he had looked so free of cares.

The place was in an uproar. Friends hugged each other, pounded each other on the back. Sándor jumped up on his chair and gave a farewell speech. His friends saluted him with tin cups of water. Kicsi sat quietly. I will be going to America, she thought. It did not seem real to her yet.

The next few days passed quickly. Vörös got her some clothes and a hairbrush and a small bag to carry them in. The day before she was to leave he gave her twenty dollars in American money.

"How much is that?" she asked. "Is that a lot?"

Vörös laughed. "Enough until you get to your cousins, anyway," he said. "Be careful with it."

She woke early the next day. The thought was already in her mind, waiting for her. America, she thought. I will be going to America today.

Around noon a bus with English words written on the side drove into the camp. The fifteen people did not need to be told that it was for them. They stood near it for two hours, until an American came up to them. A small crowd had gathered. The American called out the names.

"I'm sorry," he said to Vörös after he had called Kicsi's name. "You will not be allowed to get on the bus with her."

"All right," said Vörös. "I'll see you at the dock," he said to Kicsi.

"I know you will," Kicsi said. She boarded the bus with the American. Someone slammed the door shut, and the driver started up the engine. The crowd outside cheered them on as they drove through the gates of the camp.

The ride to the port was a short one. Kicsi looked out the window for the ship or Vörös.

They drove into the port. Vörös was there, waiting for her as she stepped down from the bus. She ran to him. "Vörös!" she said. She hugged him closely. "Oh, Vörös! Good-bye!"

"Come on," said the American. He looked at Vörös with curiosity, wondering how he had gotten from the camp to the port so quickly, then shook his head. "This way. The boat leaves in half an hour. Come on, people."

"Good-bye!" Kicsi said again. Now that she was leaving there were so many things she wanted to tell him. She had never thanked him for saving her life. She wanted to ask him if he thought the rabbi would be all right. She had never told him how much he had meant to her.

"Good-bye, Kicsi," Vörös said. She smiled. He probably knew what she would have said anyway. She turned and ran to catch up with the rest of the group.

They climbed up the ramp to the ship. It was already filled with American soldiers returning home. They ran to the railing, and Kicsi thought how odd it was that they were all so anxious to get a last look at the land they were leaving. Vörös's hair was a small dot of color among the people at the dock. He waved to her.

The ship left the dock. She waved back to him and continued to wave until he was out of sight. The coastline faded as slowly as a smile fades.

She turned and looked to the west, to America.

Fantasy Novels
from
POCKET BOOKS

___83217   THE BOOK OF THE DUN COW
   Walter Wangerin, Jr. $2.50
   *"Far and away the most literate and intelligent
   story of the year."—The New York Times*

___43131   THE WHITE HART
   Nancy Springer $2.50
   *"It has everything; a believable fantasy world...
   a lovely, poignant book."*
   —Marion Zimmer Bradley

___82912   BEAUTY Robin McKinley $1.95
   *"The most delightful first novel I've read in
   years...I was moved and enchanted."—Peter S.
   Beagle, author of THE LAST UNICORN*

___83281   CHARMED LIFE $2.25
   "An outstanding success."—Andre Norton

___83294   ARIOSTO
   Chelsea Quinn Yarbo $2.25
   *"Colorful and exciting...a vivid tapestry come
   to life...superb!"—Andre Norton*

___82958   THE ORPHAN
   Robert Stallman $2.25
   *"An exciting blend of love and violence, of
   sensitivity and savagery."—Fritz Leiber*